CW01203349

No part of this publication may be reproduced, stored in a retrieval system, or transmitted in any form or by any means, electronic, mechanical, photocopying, recording, scanning, or otherwise, without the prior written permission of the publisher, except in the case of brief quotations within critical reviews and otherwise as permitted by copyright law.

NOTE: This is a work of fiction. Names, characters, places, and incidents are a product of the author's imagination. Any resemblance to real life is purely coincidental. All characters in this story are 18 or older.

Copyright © 2020, Willow Winters Publishing. All rights reserved.

DEAN
&
ALLISON

WINTERS
USA TODAY BESTSELLING AUTHOR

From USA Today best-selling romance author Willow Winters comes an emotionally gripping, romantic suspense.

It was only a little lie.
That's how stories like these get started.
With every lie I told, he saw right through me.
I think in his heart he knew I was broken;
he felt my pain as if it was his.

And that's what changed everything.
He's the reason it all fell apart.
Sometimes it's a single moment that alters
everything in existence.
Sometimes it's the chain reaction of falling dominoes,
lined up in pretty little rows and designed so that each one
will cause more and more pain as it topples.
In a single day, everything changed,
and there's no way to go back.

I didn't know what would happen. Secrets and lies ruin
everything and I should have known better.
For the first time in I don't know how long, I wish I could
take it back. I'd take every bit of it back
if I could just be with him again.

It's Our Secret

Prologue

Allison

Say you're sorry.

As if the words mean something.

Say you won't do it again.

And pretend like you mean it.

You know you hurt me.

But that's what you wanted.

And you'll do it again ...And that's fine.

Because it's what I'm after.

There are moments that define you. As I stand outside of the house I've rented two blocks from the university's dorms, one night in particular keeps coming back to me.

That one night, six years ago, is what brought me here.

It's the night that made me who I am.

Chapter 1

Dean
Six Years Ago

"Suck my dick?" Principal Talbot asks as she stares at me with a serious expression. "Did you really tell Mrs. Pearson to *suck your dick*?" She's pissed, and that makes her question all the more comical.

Not that I wanted to cause more problems with my teachers, but come on, is it really that serious? They're just words.

She slams the window in her office shut, hushing the sounds of the students walking just outside the room. The bell rang only a minute ago, but everyone's already running from class and eager to get the hell away from Stewart High, a private school on the east side of town. That's the real problem. This place is full of uptight a-holes.

My fingers itch to be out there too, so I can sneak in a smoke before I have to go home. Everyone says it's so damn bad for you, but it's one of the only things keeping me sane. If I have to keep going through the motions and playing along, I'd rather do it stoned.

My lips twitch with the threat of a smirk but I make sure I keep a passive look on my face. I shrug and lean back in my chair as I glance over my shoulder toward her office door. "I said I was sorry."

"Do you think this is funny?" she asks me, her nostrils flaring as she stands up from her chair. She slams both hands down on her desk and leans over it to glare at me. "Do you think this is some sort of game?" With every word, her voice gets louder.

My spine stiffens, and I feel the familiar anger rising. It's not for her. Or Mrs. Pearson, for that matter. It's just that I'm so used to being screamed at. My body's ready for what's next.

I scratch my shoulder blade and try not to show anything other than a relaxed posture. I won't let any of them get to me.

"It's school, Miss Talbot. School is certainly not a game," I answer her with a solemn tone and square my shoulders, folding my hands in my lap although my foot taps anxiously on the floor. Maybe I'm baiting her but then again, maybe I don't give a fuck. I don't want to be here any more than they want me here.

It's only a matter of time until my mother or stepfather

comes through the door. I anticipate it swinging open but at the same time, I'm not sure if they'll even bother to show.

"Three schools this year, Dean. You've already been kicked out of two and now you're on your way to being kicked out of your third. Are you looking to set a record?" the principal asks me.

I don't answer her. It's rhetorical anyway.

I'm sure she has a speech prepared and I'd just hate to interrupt her.

I like being quiet. Pops used to say if you're quiet long enough, the words you finally say have more impact. Sometimes I think he only told me that so I'd shut up.

She takes her seat again and angrily clicks on her mouse as she reads through the offenses on her monitor. "Aggravated assault and drug possession, resulting in expulsion from Hamilton."

It was just pot and that fucker, Darrell, knew he was going to get his ass beat. That's what happens when you try to steal from someone. Even if it was only fifty bucks for some weed. He had it coming but then he decided to be a little bitch and rat.

Darrell can go fuck himself, Hamilton too.

She pauses to glance at me for my reaction before scrolling down what must be my school record.

I don't react and just wait for the rest of the list. It doesn't matter. None of it matters and the fact they think it does just shows how little they know.

"Destruction of public property and public indecency,"

she says and then purses her lips.

The last one makes me crack a smile and I have to hide it with my hand, covering my mouth, but it doesn't fool her.

"I'll ask you again. Do you think this is funny?" She has a pinched brow now.

"I was just showing my ass," I tell her even though I know it's going to tick her off. It doesn't matter what I say right now anyway. The end result will be the same.

"And was it funny when you told Mrs. Pearson to suck your dick?" she asks and then slips off her wire-rimmed glasses, folding them and calmly setting them down on the desk. Her blond hair remains perfectly straight.

I rest my elbow on the chair and prop up my chin to look at her. "I didn't think she'd hear it," I say. That's the truth.

One eyebrow shoots up slightly. "So it'd be okay if she hadn't heard it?"

"Not really," I say, feeling my defenses rise. "But it's not okay to call someone a failure and a waste of space either," I add, and my words are pushed through clenched teeth as I try to remember what else my algebra teacher said. I know she said "failure" at least. I know for a fact she did. All because I couldn't remember a stupid formula. If you can look it up on Google, you shouldn't be required to memorize it.

"This is about your repeated offenses, Dean. There's a clear pattern of behavior you need to address," the principal says, ignoring my statement, but there's a hint of hesitation in her response. She takes her glasses and gently puts them back on.

"You're only a freshman and your options for both public and private schools are dwindling. Do you think acting like this is going to help you deal with your issues?"

My body goes rigid at her last word. The air between us tenses and I see her expression change. It morphs to one of victory; she's finally found something that gets to me.

Principal Talbot shakes her head, the look of disappointment clearly forced. "You have no idea how much you're hurting yourself," she tells me as if she really cares.

I scoff at her and look back to the closed door.

None of them care. They just want me gone so I'm not their problem to deal with anymore.

"I can't have this type of behavior here and quite frankly, this was a favor to your mother." She looks me in the eye as she adds, "Who, I'm sure, is going to be very disappointed in you."

Her voice is stern, but that's not what gets to me. It's not what makes me rip my gaze away from hers and pick at the fuzz on the red upholstery fabric covering the armrests of my chair. It's the fact that my mother won't give a damn. Maybe she'll say she does. Maybe she'll even stand there next to that prick she married while he cusses me out for wasting his time. But does she really care? Not about me, she doesn't. She only cares about the steady supply of Xanax and the allowance he gives her.

"So, what now?" I ask, staring at Principal Talbot.

"We wait for your parents to get here—"

"*Parent*," I correct her and hold her gaze as she narrows her eyes at me. "I only have one parent." My voice almost catches. I almost let my true feelings show. But thankfully, they're mostly hidden, still buried where they belong.

"Your mother and stepfather then," she says.

I huff and focus on the lint gathered at the edge of the chair cushion, picking up the tiny pieces between my thumb and forefinger.

She'd better get comfortable. The last time this happened they never even bothered to show up.

Chapter 2

Allison

"You know you look like a ho," Sam tells me, cocking her brow like it's a question.

"Shut up," I respond dismissively, although I can't hide my smile or the laughter in my voice. It's a blip of happiness that's quickly dimmed by my rising anxiety.

After applying another coat of caramel apple lip gloss, I step back and try to pull the hem of my jean skirt down. It doesn't budge much.

"Is it too much?" I ask her the legitimate question, feeling an overwhelming need to hide and not go out tonight. My heart races as my gaze sweeps from my short skirt to the clock on the wall of my bedroom. It's one thing to think about sneaking out to meet a boy. It's another to actually do it.

Samantha rolls her eyes as she slips on a white blazer over her short red dress. It's skintight, showing off her curves and barely covering her breasts, but Sam's always flaunting her boobs.

She hit puberty first and it was damn good to her. Not so much to me.

"It's perfect," she answers with a wink.

"My mom would kill me," I mutter as I take one last look in the mirror.

"Well, your mom's not here, so there's nothing to worry about," Sam says like this is no big deal.

"I don't know," I say softly. Sam's my friend. My *best* friend. I've never kept anything from her. She already knows my stomach's acting up and I'm getting cold feet. She devoured half the pizza we ordered with the twenty bucks my mom left us for dinner. Almost all of my half is still untouched in the kitchen. I'm leaving the box on the counter. I know it'll tick my mother off to see I left it out, but I do forget to put it away every time Sam stays over, and I don't want her to think we were up to anything.

Like sneaking out.

My heart flutters with anxiousness, warning me, yet again, that this is stupid. That *I'm* stupid.

Sam's face falls slightly and she leans against my dresser as she asks, "Is it because you think Mike's going to want some?"

I huff out a sarcastic laugh and shake my head no as I stare at the ceiling to avoid her prying eyes. *Yes. Yes it is.*

"I thought you wanted to lose your V-card?" she asks me with genuine interest.

"I do," I answer immediately. "I've been thinking about how I want to do it."

"There's nothing wrong with being a virgin," Sam says, and there's a look on her face I can't quite place. Not even a trace of a smile is there. "If you want to wait, then wait."

"It's not that, I just really like him and what if he's not into it?" I swallow thickly and pick at my nail polish. Dammit. Now it's ruined. "Or what if that's not what he expects?" I say and shrug as if it doesn't matter, even though my tone doesn't match the movement.

"But you want it too, don't you?" she says. Samantha straightens her back and I can see her swallow as she looks directly ahead. "I want to know what it's like," she admits to me.

"I know. I want to know too," I tell her as if that's not obvious. "I just really like him, but if we do it tonight, is Mike going to think that I'm like ... easy or something?"

"Oh please," Samantha says and rolls her eyes. "You're thinking about this too much. If you want to do it, then do it. If you don't, then don't." She's already back to facing the mirror and fixing her necklace. "It's literally that easy," she tells me as if she's done this before when I know she hasn't, then turns toward the dresser, the tension from just a moment ago apparently all but forgotten.

"We're finally in high school, Allie," Sam says and I nod my head, although I keep my eyes on my reflection. I wish I looked like I was old enough for high school. It's clear Sam's more mature, but it's the confidence she has that I truly lack.

"Sneaking out is a rite of passage," she tells me. "I get that you like Mike and all, but just have fun tonight."

"But there's so much pressure," I say, feeling anxiety running through me again.

Sam shrugs, putting away her lip gloss and striding toward the bed for her shoes. "So what?" she asks me. "It's just a party and it's going to be a blast, and everything's going to be fine."

"Are you going to drink?" I ask her and then feel like I'm my mother.

She laughs and her eyes go wide as she says, "Duh!" While she ties up the laces to her shoes around her ankles she adds, "Are you even sure his brother got the beer?"

"He said he was getting all sorts of things." Mike's brother is a few years older and technically it's his party. Mike invited me and Sam. I was so excited when he told me, but right now I'm feeling something completely different from excitement.

"And what'd you tell him?" she asks me.

"That I like vodka," I say softly, feeling my cheeks heat with a blush and she laughs again.

"Have you ever even had vodka?" she teases me.

"Shut up," I say then push her shoulder slightly and she

just laughs some more, throwing her head back. "It's not like you've had it before either."

"Yeah, yeah. Hey, check this out," Sam says in a singsong voice as she reaches into her tote bag. It's all smooth black leather and I think she stole it from her mom's closet.

"Holy shit," I say under my breath with my eyes focused on the bottle.

"It's like a party present or something," Sam says as I pick up the bottle of red blend wine. "Hostess favor," she says, although she sounds a little uncertain. "Is that what it's called when you bring a gift to a party?" she asks me.

I set the heavy bottle back down in her bag. "I don't know," I tell her, still feeling uneasy.

"Hey, relax," Sam says and then sits in the center of my bed. It creaks under her weight. "As far as your mom knows, we're having a sleepover and tomorrow morning when she comes home, we'll be right here." She pats the bed and then grips my shoulders. "Tonight, we're going to go to Mike's house," she says and tilts her head as she emphasizes my crush's name with her broad, pearly white grin. "And we're going to be chill and cool and he's going to get to know you better."

"Maybe we can use the wine to play spin the bottle?" I say as the idea of sitting in Mike's basement and flirting makes me feel giddier than anything else has tonight.

Her smile widens and her eyes brighten. "Fucking fantastic idea," she squeals. "This is why I love you," she adds and then jumps off the bed.

"It's not because we've been friends forever?" I joke back with her.

"Best friends for life!" she answers and then twirls her long, dark brown hair around her finger. "Seriously, tonight is going to be amazing," she says with so much excitement and happiness, it's contagious.

"Can I ask you something?" I blurt out, cutting through the happiness yet again.

"Anything," Sam says instantly, looking right at me and giving me her full attention.

"Does it make me a whore if I want to have sex?" I say. "Like, even if I don't really want to be with Mike, but I just want to know what it's like?"

"Pretty sure that's normal, babe," she says with a smile. "If not, I'm fucked."

Chapter 3

Dean

My uncle's truck rumbles to a stop in front of my stepfather's house. It's the corner lot on the street, a two-story colonial with blue shutters and a porch swing right out front.

It only took my dad's death for my mother to have the house of her dreams. She even got her white picket fence.

"I don't see the point," I say to my uncle as I stare at the front door and then the driveway. "Both their cars are here." I turn to look at Uncle Rob as I speak. "If they don't want me, what's the point of even going in there?"

"You need to face the music, kid." He says it like that's why I don't want to go in there. My eyes narrow and I feel my forehead pinch.

"You don't get it. It's not just about today or yesterday. It's every day. Every single day I have to live in a house where I'm hated."

"Knock it off, Dean," my uncle says as though what I'm saying has no weight to it.

It's quiet for a long time, but my heart's pounding and all I can hear is the blood rushing in my ears. I want to get it all out. Uncle Rob's the only one who listens to me. He's the only one who gives a shit.

"Ever since Dad died," I say, and it hurts to say the words out loud as I continue, "she doesn't want me anymore."

"That's not true—" he starts to say but I raise my voice and cut him off.

"It is true!" My eyes sting and I hate it. I hate everything. I hate her the most.

"You're just angry," Uncle Rob says although he twists his hands on the leather steering wheel and looks out the window like he's judging my words. "Why can't you just be like Jack's kid?" he asks me. Jack is his friend who has two sons; one's a kid my age. "Go out and have fun. Sneak a beer, kiss a girl. Why do you have to run your mouth and make a scene?"

"It's easy for you to say," I mumble under my breath. I was going to go out with *Jack's kid* to a party tonight. I was actually looking forward to meeting Mike and a few of the guys he knows. It's been lonely since Dad died. I'm desperate enough to admit that and I finally said yeah, I'd go out. No fucking way that's happening now.

Maybe my uncle's right and that's where I should be tonight. Instead this is what I've got to look forward to.

"She didn't even cry at his funeral." My words come out hollow, matching how my chest feels. "She was already with *him*." I look him in the eye. "He slept over when Dad was in the hospital."

Uncle Rob is my mother's brother. I know he'd never say a bad word about her, but he can't deny the truth. The minute my dad got sick, my mother started counting how much she'd get from the insurance policy. Richard came next. Just like that, she moved on and didn't look back. Leaving me behind and alone when my dad died. She wasn't there with me in the hospital room and she sure as hell wasn't there after. I can't forgive her.

Uncle Rob looks uncomfortable as he runs his hand through his thinning hair and sighs.

"Why can't I just come live with you?" I practically beg him. I would give anything to get away from them. I would do anything. "You at least cared that Dad died."

"It's not that she didn't care." He doesn't say anything after that. I wait for more. For some sort of explanation that would make any of this all right, but nothing comes.

"She was happy he was going to die. All they did was fight." Although it hurts to admit the truth, there's relief in saying it out loud. Even more so because Uncle Rob doesn't deny it.

"Look, Dean, different people cope with things differently. It's hard when someone's dying and you have to handle everything."

"It was so hard that she went on smiling every day," I tell him. I don't want pretty little lies. I'm tired of living this fake-ass life my mother created. "Why can't I just live with you?" I ask him again. He's all I have. If not him, then I have no one.

"You just can't," he says like that's final and my blood chills. A sense of unease rocks through me, followed by hopelessness.

"All right then," I say and open the door to the truck, sick of arguing over pointless shit.

"It's life, kid," Uncle Rob calls after me.

"Life can go fuck itself," I tell him as I get out, making the truck rock forward and then I slam the shiny red door shut.

A sickness churns in my stomach with each step I take closer to the house.

Day in and day out. I can't do this anymore. I can't be reminded every day of how easily someone else replaced Pops. That asshole my mother cheated on my dad with expects me to listen to him? No fucking way.

I push the door open and then slam it shut from pure adrenaline, but I regret it the second the loud bang reverberates through the house.

Do I regret what I said in school? Yeah, I do. I say stupid shit, I pick fights. Maybe I am angry. Maybe I'm filled with hate.

But when I get in here, it changes.

I'm just fucking sad. I'm sad that this is my life.

The kitchen is in the center of the house and my mother's right there on a barstool, a glass of wine in her hand and the half-empty bottle on the granite countertop.

"Mom," is all I say to greet her then slip my bookbag off my shoulder, leaving it by the door. I grit my teeth when she looks up at me with daggers. She's quick to change her expression. Like she wants to hide how she really feels about me. She doesn't have to, though. I know I ruined her chance at a perfect life with Richard. The son who was an accident, forcing her to marry my father. If only I'd died with him. Then we'd all be happier.

"I can't believe you," my mother says with tears in her eyes. Or maybe they're just glossy because she's drunk. Her lips look even thinner with her mouth like that, set in a straight line.

I don't say anything; I can hear Rick getting up from the recliner in the living room.

"There you are," he says as if I'm at fault for not being here on time.

"They wouldn't let me leave till someone picked me up," I answer him with my words drenched in spite, looking him square in the eye as he storms over to me. My body tenses with the need to run or at least hold up my arms in defense.

"Is that what you got to say?" he yells at me. Rick's a former marine and he acts like it. Only angrier and usually drunk. That's one thing he and my mom have in common. His face turns red as he shouts at the top of his lungs.

The backhand comes quick, but I'm expecting it. The pain rips through my jaw, sending me backward as I hit the front door.

"You want to act like a little punk, I'll treat you like one," he spits at me. I can vaguely hear my mother screaming in between Richard's threats and the ringing in my ears.

I expected the first blow but as I stand up, I don't expect the next.

Or the one after that.

I really should have. Richard doesn't stop until I'm crying. It's not like I'm big enough to fight him, so I don't know why I try to hold back the tears. I should've just come in here looking how I feel, defeated and hopeless. Maybe then it wouldn't have lasted so long.

Metal is all I can taste when I wake up. My lips are bruised and swollen. My body's stiff from sleeping in a weird position since it hurt my face to lay on my side.

The side of my face still stings and I'm sure it looks like shit too.

I'm not going to school. Not looking like this. It would make Richard all too happy to know I had to go out with the proof that he beat the shit out of me so easily seen.

Even better for him because those asshole teachers think I deserve it. Everyone does. I'm just the piece of shit kid from her first marriage who's acting out and needs his ass beat.

That's what the last principal told my mom. That I needed my ass beat.

Maybe I do. I don't need to be sneaking out and going to parties. I just need my ass beat day in and day out until I don't feel this way anymore.

I swallow thickly and sit up in bed to crack my neck.

There's only a dresser and my bed in this room. I don't have much since we moved after Dad died. Most of my stuff I left behind. My gaze moves toward the closet, where I have two duffle bags.

My uncle doesn't want me, but that doesn't mean I can't leave. I can go somewhere. I have a little bit of cash saved up from working with Uncle Rob this past summer. I can buy a cheap car and live in it.

I might be kicked out of school; I don't know, and I don't care. I can still get a job with Nick up the street, doing landscaping. He'd hire me. He knew my dad and I've met him a few times.

I force myself off the bed quietly. The only question on my mind is whether or not I should even bother telling my mother goodbye. A sharp pain shoots from my jaw to the back of my skull, radiating there when I bend down to the bottom dresser drawer to pack up my jeans.

I don't think she'd give a fuck either way. But maybe it'd be easier for her if I don't tell her. Then she won't have to pretend like she feels a certain way. She can just be happy with Rick and her new life.

I'm not a piece of shit like he calls me. I'm not a waste of life.

I close my eyes and refuse to cry. I'll never cry because of what they think of me.

They can both go fuck themselves.

Chapter 4

Allison

My heart pounds in my chest. It's way too loud and I can't hear anything else for a moment, but as the front door to Mike's place opens wide, the music overwhelms me. With each beat, it thumps and stirs the anxiety in my stomach.

I'm really doing it.

"I'm here for Mike," I say abruptly the second the guy opens his mouth. He's tall, so tall I have to crane my neck. I don't recognize him. He's a skinny guy with long hair, and pimples line his jaw. His face is red too. It takes me a moment to realize the color in his cheeks is from drinking.

"We brought booze," Sam says, shoving the bottle of wine into the guy's chest and then walks right in like she belongs here, brushing past his shoulder.

The guy just laughs, a half-drunken sound, holding out the bottle and pointing to the back room with it. He smells like skunk and whiskey. It's what Sam's mom's boyfriend smells like all the time.

I follow Sam's lead and avoid looking around the house too obviously. But I chance a peek here and there as I move inside and slip off my coat. Every time I look around, I see someone kissing or rubbing someone else. I would feel underdressed without the protection of my jacket, but given what the other girls here are wearing, I think I fit right in. *Thank God.*

There's a lot of laughter coming from the kitchen and I'm happy Sam's steering me in that direction. Where there are people other than couples trying to dry hump in the dark corners of the living room.

I'm still looking around and taking in the place when Sam shrieks, "Mike!"

She yells over the music and makes a show of running over and hugging him. One heel kicks up in the air as she pulls Mike closer, wrapping her arm around his neck and then pointing at me. Her enthusiasm always makes me laugh. "Look what I brought you," she says playfully while I stand there tucking a stray blond lock behind my ear. The nerves settle some though when Mike smiles, and Sam lets go of him.

"Hey," I say, and it doesn't quite come out loud enough over the music, but that doesn't stop Mike from coming closer and practically yelling in my face, "I'm so glad you came."

He leans in and all I smell is beer. Probably some cheap beer that he spilled on his shirt hours ago.

"You want something to drink?" Mike asks me as he takes a half step forward, his sneaker landing on my foot. I try to play it off, but he sees me wince and backs away.

"Oh shit," he says with his forehead pinched. "You okay?" he asks and I wave him off. With my heart hammering, all the anxiousness comes right back.

It hurt like hell but with all the nerves running through me, I don't care. "I'm fine," I tell him and again, I should have spoken louder.

"Yo, Mike," the guy who answered the door yells out across the countertop and beckons Mike over. It might be his older brother; I can see a similarity with their noses beyond them both being red.

"Here," Sam says loudly, stepping into the space between the two of us and I'm grateful for her as always. She pushes a red Solo cup into my chest and I take it with both of my hands like it'll save me.

"Be right back," Mike says and I half think he slurred the last word, but the music's so loud, I could be wrong.

"We've got to catch up," Sam says as she takes a sip and then scrunches her nose and makes a god-awful face. "This tastes like piss," she says.

"Isn't it supposed to?" I ask her genuinely, but she laughs

like it's a joke.

"Okay, so, let's do a round, scope the place out and find a spot to get comfy." She lays out the plan and I nod my head, eager to do whatever she thinks is best. We decided tonight would be chill. If we're feeling it, good. If not ... we'll figure something out.

"What about Mike?" I ask her, and she gives me this look. It's a look that says I'm being stupid.

"Girl, he wants you. He'll find you, you don't have to worry about a thing." She talks as she takes my hand and leads me away from the crowded kitchen, back through the dark living room with the grinding couples having makeout sessions. We pass a set of speakers sitting on the floor and it's no wonder the bass is pounding through me. They're gigantic.

We don't stop, though. Sam leads me straight through another room that's mostly empty apart from a couple of guys smoking, then down the stairs to the basement. I follow her gratefully. Sam knows what she's doing. Or at least she looks like she does.

The door's cracked open and the lights are on. The music fades and in its place, a horde of loud and drunk voices ricochet up the skinny staircase.

"Maybe I should tell Mike we're down here?" I ask Sam as we sit on an empty sofa in the back corner of the large basement. The room itself isn't finished. It's just cinder blocks. But there's a pool table and a dartboard, plus a bar with a ton of liquor bottles lining it. Right across from the sofa is a ping-pong table with cups arranged on it.

"Babe, quit stressing," Sam tells me, draining her cup and getting up to pull her dress down. She's confident as she walks to the table and puts her cup in line with the rest. "He's going to come looking for you. Make him chase you," she says and I nod my head, although the doubt is still there. I can still barely breathe.

"I've never given you bad advice, have I?" she asks me and I know she hasn't, but she's not exactly the person I'm looking to take relationship advice from. Sam says she doesn't want a boyfriend. She just wants to kiss and that's it. But I think she's in denial. I think she lies to herself because of the shit her mom's gone through. Everyone wants to be loved. Whether they admit it to themselves or not.

That being said, she gets to kiss any boy she wants. So maybe she is right. Maybe I should make him chase me.

It only takes a couple of minutes of whispering about which nearby guy Sam likes most, before the door to the basement opens.

I'd be jealous of the attention she's getting if I didn't have my sights set on Mike. I smile into my cup as he comes down the stairs, spotting me on the couch and grinning.

"This is my cousin," Mike says while the guy behind him taps his shoulder and yells out, "We need more beer, I'll be right back." I don't pay him any attention as I scoot to my right, squishing

Sam and making a spot on the sofa for Mike to my left.

He takes it and leans in close, wrapping his arm around my shoulders and making me blush. "So, what do you guys want to do?" he asks. His voice is still loud as hell like he hasn't realized it's quieter down here.

Sam laughs and shrugs. "You want to play spin the bottle?" she says like it's a joke but I know damn well she's being serious.

"You want to?" Mike asks and looks around as if there'd be a bottle magically waiting on the coffee table. Guess we dropped the ball there.

"Why the hell not?" is Sam's answer.

"We brought a bottle to play with." I have to roll my eyes before sheepishly adding, "You know, or to drink or whatever." I hide my embarrassment by taking another sip.

"Where is it?"

"I gave it to the guy who opened the door," Sam cuts in with her hands up in an apology. "My bad," she says with a giant grin on her face. "I freaked and just handed it over." She laughs into her cup again and chugs it, emptying it and biting the rim.

"Solo cups don't work quite as well," I joke but I'm not sure Mike heard.

"So, you want to do stuff?" Mike asks and I glance at Sam, who humorlessly raises her brow.

"Getting right to it, aren't you?" she asks him flippantly,

and I smack her.

"Like what kind of stuff?" I say. I know what he means. And yes, I do. I've watched porn before. A few times with Sam, although it got a little weird, so we quickly turned that shit off. It's how she knows I like things a little different, though. "I could do stuff," I say casually as my body heats.

"Drinks!" Mike's cousin interrupts us, stomping down the stairs holding two red Solo cups and spilling beer all over the floor as he makes his way over. Sam jumps back, laughing and raising her arms in surprise and Mike's cousin shoves one of the cups into her open hand.

"Drinks," Mike bellows and clinks the plastic cups which only results in more beer being spilled and our conversation getting lost.

"Drinks," Sam mocks them, widening her eyes and imitating their excitement, but she's smiling the entire time and both the guys laugh, clinking their plastic cups with hers.

I take another sip and much to my dismay, it still tastes like piss.

Hours pass, I think. My sense of time is fuzzy.

Everything tilts when I lean against Mike. It's quieter too. Only for a moment and then it's all louder. Is this what being drunk is like?

"I just need to lie down for a sec," Sam says, gripping my arm and before I can say anything, she's already headed up the stairs.

"You want me to come with you?" I call up after her but the music is so loud that she doesn't hear me. The bass blasts through the house and makes my chest feel tight then hollow with each beat as I follow her.

"Need help?" I think I hear Mike say but when I look back, he's talking to one of the guys who's now playing beer pong.

I feel dizzy and it's all so much. "Water," I say softly and force myself to go back to the kitchen. Sam needs water. Hell, I need water too.

The smell of beer and pot hits me the second I round the corner.

Holy shit. I want to throw up.

Sam keeps moving, climbing the stairs to the second floor with both of her hands over her ears. "I'm coming, Sam," I mumble as I run to the kitchen faucet and fill two cups. One for me and one for her.

Exhaustion and a thick cloudy haze greet me as I turn the corner to go up the stairs. It takes me a moment; while I stand there, a few guys pass by me and go upstairs. Mike's cousin is one of them. The other two wait in line for the bathroom.

I watch as Mike's cousin goes into a bedroom. The door was open, but he closes it behind him.

"Hey, you going up there?" A guy's voice startles me just as I start to call out Sam's name and I swear my heart almost leaps out of my chest. My ass hits the railing as I whip around to him and spill both cups.

"Me?" I say, fear clearly evident.

"You okay?" he asks me again with a broad smile like this is funny.

But it isn't. The cups fall from my hands like I'm watching in slow motion.

"Whoa," the guy says. Some part of me dimly notices he's tall as he catches me when I tip forward. I know that I'm falling. I'm aware of it, but then it all goes black. I can hear him for a moment, asking if I'm all right and calling for help.

I guess that makes it okay, so I give in to sleep. Help is coming.

In one day, a life can change.
Or more than one.

Sometimes it's a single moment
that alters everything in existence.

Sometimes it's the chain reaction
of falling dominoes,
lined up in pretty little rows
and designed so that each one
will cause more and more pain as it topples.

In a single day, everything changed,
and there's no way to go back.

Chapter 5

Allison
Six Years Later

From the moment I laid eyes on Dean, I knew he'd be trouble.

I didn't anticipate *this*, though.

I didn't expect to let it get this far.

I didn't want him to be a casualty of my obsession.

Someone to my right clears their throat and I look down the row of people. A woman looks back at me; she's older with graying hair, wearing a thick sweater with a cowl neck that's practically swallowing the frail woman. She holds my gaze, narrowing her eyes and pressing her lips together into a flat line.

I know what she's thinking. What they're all thinking, and it makes me want to throw up.

She asked for it.
They have no idea.
No one does.
Not even Dean, as he awaits his fate.
They can judge me because I deserve it.
If I could go back, I would.

I close my eyes and try to hold back the tears, the pain. Every moment that led us here is another flaw in my armor. Picking away at my defenses as the events flash before my eyes.

When I open them, through the veil of tears scattered on my lashes, I see Dean looking back at me.

I'm so fucking selfish, and that's what pushed me over the edge.

I knew Dean would be trouble. A crimp in my plans perhaps, but I didn't think I'd fall in love.

I justified using him. I craved his touch so much that I pulled him into my web.

"I'm sorry," I mouth and Dean's expression slips.

They're right when they say I asked for it.

I didn't just ask for it, though.

No, no.

I fucking prayed for it.

Two months earlier

Fourteen boxes.

Packing and unpacking fourteen boxes takes a toll on the body. My shoulders are sore; my core feels like it's on fire.

But I'm here.

I actually went through with it and applied to this school, got in, rented a house and now I'm here.

I hear them first as I round the building that houses all the equipment for the fields. The bleachers come into sight first, followed by the men I came to see.

My hips sway a little more than before, my lips tilting up into a half smile even though my heart races. I'm so much different from the girl I was back then. Unrecognizable.

I glance at each one, taking them in as sweat glistens on their backs and chests. Most of the rugby players only have on a pair of gym shorts, ranging from blue to black to red. Their laughter drifts across the field as they huddle around the small area where all their gear is laid out.

Some of the guys play on the field of perfectly trimmed grass. Seven of them, to be exact. The field is nestled between two old brick buildings that can house hundreds of students, if not more.

Is this what college life feels like? The smell of a late summer breeze paired with jittery nerves clamber up my throat. Well, maybe the second part is just because it's me and I'm here, scoping out the intramural rugby team for the university.

Most of these guys don't take it seriously. Which is why there's no one here, no scouts or fans. A couple students sit in the grass off to the right of the bleachers, but they aren't paying attention. This rugby team isn't for show. It's just a reason to get out some aggression; judging by each of the guys' history, there's a lot of aggression here.

I knew they'd be here, practicing and putting all their goods on display.

A small hum slips from me into the late August heat as I spear my hand through my hair and let the wind push it out of my face and off my shoulders.

It doesn't take long for one of them to notice me walking a little closer than I should.

The field backs up to woods behind the buildings and the only reason I'd be walking out here on this side of the field is for them. And now they know it.

The guy closest to me tilts up his chin as he asks, "What's going on?"

The rest of them quiet down when I walk up to the bleachers and take a seat, letting my bag fall into the grass as I rest against the metal. I'm in jeans, so I spread my legs just a bit as I lean forward, my body language suggestive. Yeah, nothing like the girl I used to be.

"I just came to see the game," I say sweetly and let my eyes drift from the tall blond with broad shoulders, to the darker brunette with a full sleeve tattoo down his left arm.

"No game today, sweetheart," a man at the far end of the group tells me, but I don't turn to look that way.

"There's always a game," I say. "I'm Allison," I add, flirtation evident in my voice.

"Well, hello," the closest guy—the dark blond, or dirty blond as I like to call it—says and strides closer to me, taking a seat to my left but far enough away that I'm still comfortable. "I'm Daniel," he tells me.

"I know," I say and then bite down on my lower lip. "Daniel, the one with the Irish temper," I add, quoting his bio from the website for the frat that sponsors the team. I look at the remaining six men on the field. Daniel isn't a student, just a guy listed as "occasional manager" on the website. I imagine it's an inside joke. It took hours to look them all up and Daniel definitely caught my eye. I'm not into blonds normally, but I certainly noticed him.

"James has the beard," I say to the man with the neatly trimmed facial hair and then add, "Don't shave it or I might forget who you are." That gets a laugh from them. He's classically handsome, but only slightly above average looking.

I finally take a look at the guys on the fringe. I expect to feel a certain way, but what's a complete surprise is how my gaze is caught, trapped by a beast of a man. His eyes pierce through me, pinning me in place. It takes a moment for me to even register any other defining feature. I can practically feel his sharp jawline covered in stubble that would be rough to the touch. His hair is nearly black and just long enough to grip at the top, but shorter on the sides.

His shoulders ... broad enough to trap me under him. *Thud*. One beat is all my heart gives me. Then the poor thing plays dead.

"I don't know yours," I say, feeling my pulse pump a little harder. My body heats with the way he looks at me. Like he's looking me up and down, trying to undress me with that sharp hazel gaze of his.

There's something different about him. The air around him is tense. And I'm grateful for the distraction.

"Dean," he tells me and his expression stays hard. I'd almost say it's cold but that's so wrong. Plenty of heat is there, a heat of defiance. And something else, something dangerous.

He's the type of man who gives you chills even as he heats up everything else.

The kind of man you know you're supposed to stay away from because he'll ruin you without thinking twice ... The kind my dreams are made of.

A small smirk lifts up Dean's lips as if he can read my mind. As if the dirty thoughts in my head are what his dreams are made of too.

"We're just finishing up a workout," Daniel says and I nod as he adds, "We're getting ready to party." His voice is deep, but Dean's is deeper.

"Damn, I was really looking forward to your practice," I answer him with a pout, finally ripping my eyes away from Dean. Back to the entire point of being here.

"You want to come?" Daniel asks, inviting me to whatever party they're having, and I shake my head before peeking at Dean. He's still watching me with that hunger in his eyes. "Come on, I know you do," he teases and the playfulness in his voice makes me smile. He's cute in a charming way.

"Not today," I say, my voice coming out a little smaller than I'd like.

"Suit yourself," Daniel says and stands up, walking to where he's laid his bag on the ground. "If you change your mind, come on down to Broom Street." He smiles with a warmth that's inviting. "It's going to be fun," he adds.

A few guys let out a rough laugh, deep and low. "You'll know which house is us," one of them says.

I keep finding my gaze drifting toward Dean's and each time I do, his intense stare is on me. I didn't come here for him. A little flirtation here and there is all I was aiming for, but the way he looks at me is doing something to me that I can't deny.

He's bad for me. But I can't help what I want.

Chapter 6

Dean

I like how she's acting like she doesn't recognize me. The way she twirls the pen in her brunette curls, looking up at the professor then slipping the tip of that pen between her teeth.

Fucking tease.

Her name's Allison. I love the way it slips off my tongue.

I didn't look at her twice the first day we sat in this room. But I noticed when we crossed paths in the building next door, the one with the cafeteria. And I noticed when she started walking away from campus and toward the houses down Connell Street, only two blocks down from Broom Street.

The tiny glances and the subtle way she shifts her thighs each time she sees me ... that got my attention even more.

Maybe it's the curve of her waist or the way her lips are almost always just slightly parted. But something drew me to her and now the idea of her on her knees in front of me as her lips open wider to take the head of my dick is all I can think about.

And then she can treat me to the same sucking she's doing to that pen right now.

Maybe she's got my attention because Chem 201 is boring as hell.

Or maybe it's because Little Miss Allison looks as though she'd be down for a dirty fuck, but she's avoiding me at all costs.

Like right now. She's got to know I want her. Maybe she likes the chase.

All she's doing is skimming that pen across her bottom lip, making my dick twitch with need.

"And you?" the professor asks, his voice directed this way. I'm one row behind and two seats to the left of her.

"I'm sorry?" she questions Professor Grant, caught off guard. My lips curl up into a smile, although I hide it behind my fist as I brace my elbow against the desk. Yeah, I know I'm getting to this broad. Whether she wants to let on that I am or not.

"What's the constitution of the nucleus of an atom?" he repeats his question, and my brow raises slightly. We're only five days into the semester and this class meets Mondays, Wednesdays, and Fridays. Week one is too fucking early for this shit.

"Electrons and neutrons," she answers hesitantly.

"Wrong," the professor's voice rings out and Allison purses her lips. The pen in her hand taps on the textbook in front of her as the class know-it-all pipes up, not even waiting to be called on.

The answer is protons and neutrons, not that I give a shit. My major's undecided for now but there's zero chance of me going into chemistry for a career.

I lean over, feeling the metal bar separating our rows pushing into my ribs.

"Maybe you should pay attention." I whisper my first words to Allison, and she finally looks at me.

She gives me a side-eye paired with an asymmetric grin and I give her a charming smile back before relaxing into my seat.

After the professor turns his back to us, ranting about something he's scribbled on the chalkboard, she looks over her shoulder toward me.

Her teeth sink into her bottom lip and she blushes, peeking at me and then once again pretending to pay attention to him and not me.

That only makes me want her more. I know she's thinking about me. I want to know exactly what she's daydreaming about. That way I can make it come true.

I know she didn't recognize me yesterday on the field, but I recognized her. She's fucking gorgeous, assertive. Doesn't know what's in an atom, though. I smirk and act like I give a shit about what's on the board when Professor Grant turns around and looks right at me. I even nod for his benefit.

The desk groans as I readjust in my seat and get another glance from Allison when the lecture continues and his voice drones on.

Not a lot of women approach a group of men with confidence. There's a shyness but also a sense of playfulness in this one that I like. It's something I want to explore and judging by the way she acted yesterday, compared to how she's been in class the last two times, quiet and reserved, I'm guessing she'd like to explore some shit too.

The large clock above the door ticks by so damn slowly as I wait for class to end. *Tick, tick, tick.* Every time Allison puts that pen into her mouth, my dick gets a little harder. She lets it roll down her bottom lip and she'd be lying if she said she wasn't doing it on purpose.

By the time two o'clock hits, I'm hard as fucking steel.

I stay in my seat as everyone around me packs up, my eyes still on my prey.

As she closes her book, she deliberately avoids my gaze again.

"I thought you'd be shy," I say as the person to my right leaves, blocking my view of Allison for only a fraction of a second. She sets the heavy textbook into her backpack and zips it up, all the while looking at me with an expression that tells me she doesn't know how to answer.

"When I saw you the last two classes," I tell her and then close my book, "you seemed shy and not at all like you were yesterday."

"Is that right?" she asks, tucking her hair behind her ear and setting her bag back down on the floor. She turns in her seat to face me and says, "I didn't know we had a class together. I guess it was just nerves."

"You didn't look too nervous yesterday."

"Why do you say that?" she asks me, but there's a spark of mischievousness in her eyes. It makes my smile widen.

"It seemed like you wanted something particular."

"And what would that be?" she says. I notice how her chest rises and falls with her shallow breathing.

I lean forward and lower my voice. "Can I tell you something?"

"What?" Her lips stay parted just slightly and she stares at me with curiosity.

"I called dibs when you left," I tell her. It's not true. After she left, her hips swaying and a small bit of that shyness returning when she saw me watching her fine ass walk away, all that the guys were talking about was how much ass they're going to get in college.

Her ass, any ass. It doesn't matter to them. But this one I'd noticed before. This one is obviously in need. So when she left the field, the vision of her soft lips stayed in my mind.

"Did you really call dibs?" she asks me and then shakes her head like I'm ridiculous.

They don't get *this* ass. Not until I get my fill first.

"Yeah," I tell her and look around the now empty room. "Where's your next class?"

"I don't have anything else after this," she says.

"Me neither," I tell her and she throws her head back, laughing.

"You're such a liar," she says, calling me out with a voice full of humor. Her genuine smile grows and a beautiful shade of pink colors her cheeks. "You want to get into my pants badly enough that you'd miss your next class?"

My adrenaline spikes. "How'd you know?" I ask her.

"Your schedule's right there," she says and rolls her eyes. She grabs the paper off my desk and verifies that she's right before tossing it back to me.

"It's right next door but you're going to be late if you wait any longer," she says confidently and stands up, swinging her backpack over one shoulder.

"It can wait if you want to get out of here," I offer her.

"You're shameless," she says and then she grips the strap of her bookbag and asks me softly, "You think I'm that easy?"

"I think you want it. You might be afraid to get it, though."

Her expression slips just slightly, so quickly I almost don't see it and I second-guess my approach. "I think you know what you want." I speak clearly and wait for her light green eyes to reach mine. "I fucking love that."

"Oh yeah?" she says, her confidence returning and the air between us heating again. The tension between us thickens as I stand up, closing the small space that separates us. She stays still, letting me get close enough to touch her. I don't, though. I can make her want the chase too.

"Yeah, and I know what I want too," I tell her and lean forward, so fucking close, but she turns her shoulder to me, brushing against my chest and arm as she walks away, leaving my heart beating hard.

"Well right now, I want to go home, Dean," she says over her shoulder.

"Love the way you say my name too," I tell her and she pauses in the doorway. "I can make it sound even better when you scream it."

She lets her head fall back with a feminine peal of laughter. "You really are shameless."

"We have a game tonight," I say quickly before she can leave. It grabs her attention and she looks back at me. "On the field. Nothing big, but you should come."

"You're inviting me to your game?" she asks me with a hint of a smile. It makes her happy, I can tell.

"I am and I'm going to win you over," I say, picking up my bag and following her out of the room. "I know you want me," I tell her, cocky as fuck.

"We'll see," she says softly, letting her gaze roam down my chest to my cock, then back up to my eyes. "Not today, though. Get to class," she commands, and her voice hardens.

"Bossy," I tease her as she turns left. I debate following

her. But now's not the time. She's just the right mix of shy and curious, but also confident and sexy as hell. I watch her disappear before turning right to go to my next class. "All right, Allie Cat, round one goes to you," I say lowly.

My dick's still hard and there's a trace of a smile left on my lips.

College just got that much better.

Chapter 7

Allison

I shouldn't be thinking about Dean Warren.

I definitely shouldn't be going to this game for him.

And the smile on my lips when he does a double take over his shoulder, as I sit on the uncomfortable metal bleachers, that really shouldn't be showing.

He's a mistake waiting to happen.

The cockiness and arrogance mixed with the hard edge in his eyes are what tell me that much. As if a simple look wasn't enough to warn me off.

He's the type of guy who will force you against a hard wall, lift your skirt and tear off the thin fabric beneath it with a forceful tug. The type of guy who will hold you there while you scream as he takes you harder and harder.

He's the type of guy my mother told me I should stay away from.

Good thing I stopped listening to my mother years ago.

He's a mistake I've made before. Not just once or twice, and you'd think I'd have learned my lesson by now. Maybe I can blame it on insta-lust.

My heart slams against my rib cage, hating that I'm in such denial.

He's a distraction. Dean is a distraction who could ruin everything. And maybe that's why I can't resist him. *Do I really want to do this?* I clear my throat and square my shoulders as my shoes sink into the grass. The urge to turn around without looking back is strong.

I was headed this way anyway.

The thought makes me smile. It almost makes me think that it's even okay. That everything was meant to work out like this.

It's a little late for me to be starting college but hey, being thrown to the wolves when you're legally allowed to drink isn't the worst thing in the world. I'm only a year behind and I have plenty of catching up to do. I'm shocked at how easy it is to get back into the student life. I graduated high school, went to community college for a year, then dropped out when Grandmom got sick only. One year later and I'm picking up the pieces, but blending in has been easier than I thought it would be.

"Go State!" I yell out and clap after setting my bag down on the ground.

There are maybe a dozen people scattered throughout the stands.

The field is small, as is the university. No one comes here because of their athletics program, that's for damn sure.

It's just an intramural team and there's not even a real game today. It's basically some guys fucking around. Shirts versus skin and lucky for me, Dean happens to be one of the shirtless players.

Just as I let my eyes admire his body, he jolts forward and tackles the shit out of another guy—Daniel, I think. It's only when the guy stands up that I confirm it's Daniel. Oh my. I'm not going to lie; this isn't as bad as I thought it would be.

Rugby's a violent sport.

The violence is what attracts me. It's like playing with fire … and that's what I came to do.

The men crash together, and I keep staring at one in particular. They slam into each other, brutalizing one another, all in the name of a good game.

It's not a game to me. There's too much at stake to call it that.

I can't watch, but I also can't rip my eyes away.

Thud. Thud. My heart pounds harder and harder as the memories slowly come back to me, and I need to shove them away. Hide them, bury them deep down inside.

Deep breaths. Calming breaths.

It only takes a glance in the wrong direction at the wrong time and it all comes flooding back.

I force a small smile to my lips, unclenching my fists and only just now realizing how my nails dug into my skin. As I reach for the water bottle in my bag, I lift my gaze back to the field, only to find Dean staring at me. The grim look proves he was watching me and knowing that, I can't breathe.

It's like he can see right through me. I'm saved by the loud clap of someone else sitting in the bleachers behind me. Our connection is broken and only then is my body willing to play it off. To relax and pretend like it's all right.

Dean is like a drug to a recovering addict.

He makes me question everything. All the things I have planned.

He makes me want to run but at the same time, he paralyzes me.

Five more minutes and I'll leave, I promise myself.

I'm waiting for them to break up their huddle and keep playing, but that's not what happens.

The bottle nearly slips from my grasp as Dean strides over to me and the other guys line up on the field without him.

Dean takes a seat next to me and I'm instantly hit with his warmth and masculine scent. His sweat smells sweet and addictive.

"What are you doing?" he asks me.

"I was watching this hot guy who has a crush on me play this dumb sport," I say and fail to hide my smile as I add, "He gave up, though."

He chuckles and that gorgeous smile flickers onto his face. "I wasn't sure you were going to stay, and I wanted to make sure I let you know before you left that we're having a party tomorrow night at James's place," he tells me.

"First a game and now a party?" I ask him, taking another swig from the bottle and fiddling with the plastic cap in my left hand. "You like asking me on dates, don't you?"

He shrugs and glances at the guys on the field, but I keep my eyes on him. "I think you'll like the party better. I'll be able to give you a little more attention."

I roll my eyes and almost turn back to the field, but I stop myself. I don't want to look that way right now.

"You think if you get a little alcohol in me, you'll have a better chance?" I ask him, although I keep glancing behind him to the right side of the field to see if any of the guys are watching us.

Dean makes a show of looking over his shoulder in the direction I keep checking out before shifting to block my view and standing a little closer. His broad shoulders tower over me. This is the second time he's been this close to me, and it only makes me want to be closer.

I can smell his unique, sexy scent and feel the heat in his eyes when I meet his gaze. It's a heady combination. To have someone you're innately drawn to so close. To know they want something you also want. But to also know with complete certainty it's the last thing you should do. The temptation heats the air around us and turns everything to a blur of white noise.

"I don't need a better chance," he finally answers me, his eyes narrowing. "I already told you, I want you and I'm not going to stop until you're screaming my name just how I want to hear it."

"So confident," I say, although it comes out differently than I'd planned. It was supposed to be sarcastic but instead, there's a hint of reverence.

"Come to the party," he tells me like it's a command and ignores the voices on the field. The ones calling out for him to head back. I use that as my excuse to leave.

"You go play, and I'll see you this weekend," I answer him without thinking.

"You're leaving already?" he asks me and I nod.

"I've got shit to do now that I have plans for tomorrow." He likes that; I can tell by the way he smiles, and it does something to me. Something it shouldn't.

"Twenty sixteen Broom Street," he tells me, but I already know the address.

Chapter 8

Dean

"So, what do you think about college?" Dr. Robinson asks me. He lowers his thick, horn-rimmed glasses and sets them down on the notepad in his lap. "Is it a good change?"

My right ankle rests on my left knee as I sit back, running both my hands through my hair. "Yeah, it's different. It's good."

"Talk to me about it," he says, prodding me for more. He's good at that.

"I don't want to disappoint Jack, and I'm grateful. I still don't know what I want to do, though."

"Well, it's only been a week and I'm sure Mr. Henderson wouldn't have sponsored you if he thought you'd disappoint him."

"We all know it was a favor to my uncle. I live off favors,"

I say flatly, although I don't look him in the eye. My gaze is on the ceiling fan in the center of the room. When I close my eyes, I can just barely feel the soft breeze. I wonder if anyone else in college feels as lost as I do. Like this is their last chance. I've been on my last chance for years now, so maybe this is my version of normal.

"Do you think you don't deserve it?" he asks me and I lower my gaze so I can meet his eyes. His expression is one of curiosity.

"A free ride to college isn't something I ever thought I'd get."

"And anger management? How about that?" he says, shifting in the seat of his dark brown leather chair. "Is that something you thought you'd get?"

A low chuckle makes my shoulders shake. "Yeah, that makes sense to me," I say with a grin.

"How do you think this is working for you?"

"I feel good," I answer him and hope the gratitude comes through. "It's nice to just say the shit I'm thinking."

"Have you thought more about my last suggestion?" he asks me and I shake my head.

"Well, yeah, I've thought about it," I say, correcting myself, realizing I was answering no to the wrong question. "I'm not doing it, though."

I left my mother's house six years ago. From there I survived by hopping from friend to friend. Crashing at my uncle's when he'd let me. I haven't gone back to that hellhole my mother calls home and I don't plan on it.

She doesn't want me there, so why would I?

"You don't think your mother would be interested in seeing your progress?" he asks.

"I don't see it as progress," I say.

"Why's that?"

The answer is obvious. College isn't a job. There's no worth to it. No value in it.

I don't know what the hell I'm doing with my life. I'm not offering anything to anyone. I'm just ... here. How is that progress? It's better for me, don't get me wrong. It's not better for anyone else, though.

"I don't see the point to it." I pause and swallow thickly, bending forward and repositioning so my elbows are on my knees. I can feel the stretch through my back, loosening my tight shoulders and coiled muscles. "I like the team, I like the gym."

"The physical release?" he asks me, and I can't help but think of Allison.

My fingers interlace as I nod. "Yeah, the physical release," I say and look up at him to keep from thinking about what I'd do to her if I got the chance.

"And you think you need this physical release?"

"I need something," I answer quickly. I don't tell him the truth. About how all that shit puts me on edge. How it makes me need more. How that alone will never be enough. Deep inside I know it, but I don't admit it.

"Anything else?" he asks as if he read my mind.

"Nothing yet," I tell him and falter, but decide to talk about her. Why the hell not? It's better than talking about my emotions. How easily the hate comes out. How I can't control the shit I say and the shit I do sometimes.

Well, maybe not so much that I can't, but that I don't want to.

"There's this girl," I start telling him while I pick up a fidget block from the glass coffee table. It's pointless. A block of buttons and switches that do nothing, but it keeps my hands busy.

"She's real flirtatious and cute. We have chemistry together." After seeing his brow raise, I add to clarify, "The class." It's quiet as he scribbles on the notepad.

"I keep running into her," I tell him. "I guess she's on my mind because of that."

"You're seeing her?"

I shake my head. "Nah, I wouldn't say that."

"Have you been physical?" he asks me.

I tell him the truth, but in my head? Fuck yeah. Imagining getting her under me has been a good distraction.

That second day of class, she was dressed in a tight shirt and a short little skirt.

The shirt wasn't see-through like I was fantasizing about, but with the blue plaid skirt, she was working that schoolgirl look. She did a damn fine job of it too.

All during class, all I did was think about everything I could do to her. How I could bend this shy girl over the desk so easily.

Every time she readjusted in her seat, I imagined being behind her, lifting her ass up and positioning her just how I wanted. I could hear how the desk would scrape across the floor as I pounded into her.

It only took a few minutes before I was rock hard and eager to see just what I'd have to do to get under that skirt.

The second class was over, Little Miss Brunette, my personal tease, was gone before I even shoved my notebook into my bag.

"Why do you think you're drawn to her?" he asks me, pulling me from the explicit thoughts running through my head.

"She's got a mouth on her," I reply and think I should elaborate on how it's what she says, more than her body, that gets me going. Hell, either way you look at it is accurate.

"So, you're going to pursue her?" he asks me, picking up the notebook again to jot something down.

If by pursue her, he means fuck her until my cock is spent, then yes, that's what I'm planning.

I don't tell him that though, I just nod my head once when he looks up.

"So, you have your workout sessions, your rugby team, you have a love interest," he lists then pauses as I snort, but I clear my throat and gesture for him to continue.

"Have you thought about changing your major?" he asks

me then adds, "It's just something to keep in mind. I know it's still early, but undecided is not exactly what you want from this experience, is it?"

"No, I definitely want to figure shit out," I say and toss the fidget block back on the table. "I feel wound tight, like I just need something."

"What do you need?" he asks me.

"I don't know," I tell him honestly. "I want to know, though." I nod my head, swallowing back the disappointment, the fear that I'll never know what I need to get over this anger. Or worse, that it's just too late.

I have a good idea why I'm like this. It doesn't take a genius to figure it out. But I don't know how to change and even worse, I don't know what I'll be like when I do change. And that scares the shit out of me.

According to the good doctor, college is where you go to find out who you are. So far, I've learned I'm a man who has a vivid imagination when a sexy piece of ass wears a short plaid skirt to class. There's a shocker.

Chapter 9

Allison

"Your flowers are dying," I say out loud although there's no one else here. My fingertips brush against the soft petals on a single bloom that's still alive. "This one will be dead soon too," I say and pause, letting my hand fall. "This window will be good for you, though," I add as I water the first plant and then the next in the large bay window. It faces east and there's plenty of sun.

This was my grandmother's therapy. Plants need to be talked to, she used to tell me. I thought she was crazy, but I did it anyway.

And when she gave me a violet of my own, I took her advice. Shame the thing's dying. Maybe I should talk more.

My throat feels dry and itchy when I stand back, no longer busying myself.

"Miss you," I whisper. "You wouldn't be so proud of me if you were here, though," I say. I spent most of my first year out of high school with my grandmother. She needed someone and I did too. She'd have liked this house, I think. I'm happy I was able to rent it. The price is good, but the location is everything. It's exactly where I need it to be.

For the longest time, Grandmom was the only one I talked to. I'd work at the bakery, take care of Grandmom and then go home to sleep. It kept me busy and somehow my grandmother rubbed off on me. Over time, it became easier to refuse to let anyone in.

Maybe it's because she's a hard woman too. Or was. She knew how hard it is to give even a little piece to anyone. Opening up a little inevitably means breaking down.

She was tough and she showed me how to survive being this way.

But now she's gone and I'm here all alone.

The click of the air conditioner is met with the curtains swaying. They're bright white with bluebirds scattered across them. This is the only area in the entire house that's decorated; it's supposedly the dining room, but the table that came with the sparsely furnished place is strangely small for such a large room. And I don't have any desire to put in any effort anywhere else. I can't stand to be here any longer than I need to be.

At that thought, I head to the kitchen for a cup of tea.

The electric kettle is Grandmom's too. Another reminder. The plants, the tea ... well, maybe that's it.

Standing at the laminate countertop, I look around the mostly empty kitchen. I don't even have cutlery. But that's okay, I don't think I'll be staying here long. "I brought your plants, though," I say out loud like a fucking lunatic. Does it make it any better if I know I'm unwell? I tell myself it's for the plants. Talking out loud to my dead grandmother is so the plants can grow. Yeah ... okay.

The kettle beeps and the light goes off, so I go about my business. Tea and then research. I pause after pouring the hot water into the porcelain cup, remembering Dean.

He's definitely a man who leaves an impression. I smile into the tea, drinking it unsweetened and loving the warmth as it flows through my chest. Dean's also a wanted distraction.

"You'd hate him, Grandmom," I say with my eyes closed. "Or maybe not," I say then shrug and remember how she gave me the advice to get over one man by getting under another. It was only a joke to her but I think she was onto something.

With each sip of tea, I think about Dean. His large, strong hands. The way he likes to pretend he's not wound tightly when it's obvious he is. The hot tea is a soothing balm, but getting rid of this wound called Dean requires more than a mere hot drink. I should know.

Just as I'm starting to relax, just as I feel a bit sane, my phone rings in the living room. My pace is slow, and all the good feelings are replaced with ice.

There's only one person who calls me and I don't want to talk to her. I will, but all she'll get are the pieces of me that remain. The remnants of who I used to be. She made her choice, and now we both have to deal with it.

I take my time tossing the used tea bag into the trash, where it hits an empty box of hair dye. I absently twist the brunette curl dangling in my face around my finger as I walk to my phone. I don't want to look like the girl I once was. I don't want to be her anymore. Dyeing my hair helps.

"Hello," I answer the phone, setting the cup down on the floor and sitting cross-legged to look out the sliding doors at the back of the house.

"You answered." My mother sounds surprised, and maybe she should be. It's been a long time since I've heard her voice.

"What's going on, Mom?" I ask her, feeling a sense of loneliness I haven't felt in a while. Maybe it's not the anger that keeps me at a distance from her. Maybe it's just because she's a reminder of what happened.

"I wanted to let you know I bought you a sofa." Her voice has a feigned sense of happiness to it. Like she can pretend we're okay and one day we'll be back to normal. "I need your address so I can send it. And a TV stand too. And if you need anything else …"

"Mom, you didn't have to do that," I tell her simply. It hurts when I talk to her. Physically hurts. Because I still love her, but I hate her too. I can't forgive myself and she's the one who led me down that path. I'd rather hate her than hate myself.

"I wanted to, and I know that you quit working when ... she passed away four months ago, so money must be tight. If you need any ..." my mother falters then continues, "I don't know what you have saved, but I can send you—"

"I'm fine." I hated that job at the bakery anyway. It was just killing time and numbing the truth of what I needed to do. It's not like I was going anywhere running the register.

"Will you let me send them to you?" she asks me and it's the anguish in her voice that makes me cave.

It's not that I want to hurt my mother. I know she's in pain like I am. I just don't want to be around her. I don't want to forgive her because then it would be like what happened was okay.

And it never will be. Never.

"Sure, I'll text my address to you," I agree mostly out of guilt.

"Thank you," she says, and I think she's crying on the other end of the phone.

"Are you okay?" I ask her.

"I just miss you; I miss your grandmother too."

"I miss her too ... She's in a better place now." I say the words, but I don't mean them. They're only for my mother's benefit. If it wasn't for my grandmother's death, I'm not sure my mother and I would even have a relationship. It's been six years of hardly saying a word to each other. For most of them, I lived under her roof. Both of us keeping busy and ignoring each other.

I remember when I started sneaking out how she pretended I wasn't.

I kept pushing and she let me get away with murder. She didn't want to fight me. She didn't want a reason for us to argue. It's the guilt that does that. Either that or the shame.

"I have to go, Mom," I tell her as I watch the leaves on the trees behind my house gently sway with the wind. It wasn't until I moved in with my grandmother that my mom admitted our relationship was strained. She likes to pretend, but I don't have the strength for that. Or maybe it's the other way around.

"Well, call me," she tells me hurriedly before I can hang up. "If you need anything."

"I will," I answer, although that's not going to happen. I already know that and I'm sure she does too. "Thank you for the furniture," I add. "I really appreciate it."

"You don't already have anything, do you?" she asks me. "It didn't seem like you packed much."

"No, I didn't. Thank you."

I end the call as fast as I can. I know Mom wants to talk. But she's saying all the wrong things.

Then again, I am too.

I'm holding back; I know that much is true.

I know what I need to do, but it hurts to think about it. It's going to change everything, and I don't know who I'll be after it happens.

And that's what scares me the most. When this is over, I don't know what will be left.

Chapter 10

Dean

Foam spills over the rim of the red Solo cup as I fill it. It falls into the bucket with the rest of the spilled beer.

The last time I had a drink from a keg was at a party for my uncle's company. He's in construction and so was I until I got set up with Jack Henderson, Kev's uncle and my uncle's friend. That beer was in celebration of hard work. This beer is just because we can drink all night and not give a shit.

And it's the first of many to come. Cheers to that.

I down the cold beer and put my cup back under the spigot to fill it up again.

A pretty little thing sidles up next to me, letting out a small laugh when she bumps her ass on my thigh. Like it was an accident and she was just reaching for the corkscrew on the countertop in front of us.

"My bad," she says with a smile and throws her hair over her shoulder as she grabs the corkscrew. She looks back at me one more time as she walks away in her tight faded jeans and tank top that rides up, showing off the tramp stamp on the small of her back. It's a tribal design around a rosebud. Probably something she picked off the wall of the tattoo shop.

"No problem," I tell her and take another sip as she walks off. She's cute but the one girl I want to see hasn't come through the front door. I've been sitting here all night long, the beer right next to me. My back's against the counter as I face the front door watching everyone shuffle in and out, with the night sky getting darker, the music louder and everyone in here drinking more and more.

James's family house is the perfect location for these parties. Right off campus and it's within walking distance to the dorms but also the frat and sorority housing. All you have to do is follow the train tracks up the block and it leads you right here. Walking on the railroad tracks isn't the best thing to do when you're drunk, but at least you can't take a turn down the wrong street.

Just as I down the rest of the beer and think about heading to the pool room in the back, the front door opens and in walks Allison. Her pouty lips are pulled into a curious smile as she tucks her clutch under her arm and closes the door. I like how she leans against the door, taking in the place before pushing off and heading this way.

My eyes follow her, waiting for the moment when she sees me. Her hips sway in the most tempting rhythm as she glances over her shoulder, moving the hair behind her ear and exposing more of her neck. With her black dress and red lips, she's elegantly beautiful, but it's tainted.

By the way she walks.

By the expression on her face.

By the way she halts, sinking her teeth into her bottom lip and looking me up and down. I smirk as she lets her eyes roam and then stalks toward me.

"You're late," I tell her and that only makes her laugh.

"I come when I'm ready," she says in a sultry voice. She eyes the keg and then where I'm standing, which is right in the fucking way.

I'm only an observer as she takes a cup off the counter and then slips between me and the keg, settling her ass right against my dick. She takes her time, bending over as much as she can while she fills her cup.

My dick stiffens and the second it does, she winks over her shoulder at me.

Taking a sip of beer, she scoots out from between me and the keg and then turns to face me. I wouldn't have been surprised if she'd walked right out of the kitchen, leaving me hanging again.

"Oh, and I always come first too," she says, holding up her cup and arching her brow. "That's one of my rules."

"You're a tease," I tell her as my pulse quickens. She holds my gaze and those pale green eyes flicker with heat.

More people filter into the room, a horde of girls all stumbling in their heels and spilling their drinks, laughing as they crowd the kitchen.

Allison doesn't object when I grab her hand and pull her out of there, heading to the living room on the right.

"It's loud," she says, raising her voice and tugging on my hand, stopping me from taking her to the back.

"There's a rec room this way," I tell her and move my hand around her waist to keep her moving. I love how she doesn't protest.

She walks with me through the living room, past the speakers, through the back hall and straight out to the pool room. There are a few arcade games too in the back and there are more people waiting around them than there are playing pool.

I tilt my chin up at Daniel as he stands up, holding the pool cue in his hands and watching the six ball sink straight into a back pocket. He's an all right guy. Out of all the guys, he's the one I've clicked with most since I moved here. He's an outsider in a lot of ways. Like me. And I know he only hangs around because of some dealings he's got going on under the table. It's not my business and I stay out of it. It's as simple as that.

The second he sees my Allie Cat, he smiles wider. It's a

triumphant grin and it matches the one on my face when he gives me a nod.

"Aw," Allison says as she walks toward the side wall where the barstools are set up, "I thought it was going to be empty." She smirks after saying it and her eyes light up with mischief.

"Like I said, you're a fucking tease."

"And you like it," she says back then lifts the cup to her lips. She doesn't take her eyes off me, though.

I have to readjust my dick in my pants before I can sit down and watch the pool game.

"Admit it," she says, her voice a bit stronger than I expected.

"Admit what?" I ask her.

"That you like it."

"Yeah, so what if I do?" I tell her with confidence. "You already know that."

"I just like hearing you say it," she says and shrugs her small shoulders, making the dip in her collarbone that much more pronounced. The second she turns away from me, her cheeks color a beautiful shade and her legs sway. Like she's shy all of a sudden, just hearing that I like her. I'll keep that in mind, how easy it is to make her look like that. I like seeing this timid side of her.

"What else do you like to hear?" I ask her, and she just smiles slightly into her cup, tilting it back and taking a larger gulp. "I'll tell you whatever you want." My offer goes with the rest unspoken. I'll give you what you want, you give me what I want. It seems fair as fuck to me.

"Is this the room?" she asks me curiously and tilts her head.

"The room?" I ask her to clarify and she slips her hand up my shirt. Her fingers tickle along my skin as she leans forward. "You know," she says then licks her lower lip and adds, "the room where everything happens. Or is there an empty bedroom?" As she leans back, she takes her touch with her, leaving me wanting more and wishing there was a room to take her fine ass.

"I'm in the dorms, I don't stay at the frat house." She seems surprised by that, so I fill her in. "Kev's uncle is paying my ride here to keep me out of trouble and Kev thought I'd make a good addition, but this isn't really my style."

"Then what is your style, Dean Warren?"

"Doing whatever I have to, so I can hear you say my name just how I've been dreaming."

Her delicate simper widens, and I take a chance, setting my hand on her thigh.

"Oh, the first move has been made," Allison says sarcastically but leaves my hand right where it is. She shifts on the barstool and it makes the thin fabric on her already short dress ride a little higher. My fingers are so fucking close to the hem, and just beneath that, the apex of her thighs.

"You like it," I say and then pinch the hem of her dress and pull it down as much as I can before taking the cup from her hand.

"Hey, I wasn't done," she says and sulks but I ignore her, walking to the bar and grabbing the vodka and a can of Sprite. I hold it up for her to see and her eyes light up.

"I guess that'll do," she says with a devilish glint in her eyes.

I grab the whiskey for me and pour my own drink in a glass.

"No ice?" she asks when I hand her the drink I've fixed her and stand in front of her, effectively caging her in.

"You want ice in yours?" I ask her.

"I mean in yours," she says softly, her voice a bit huskier than it was a moment ago. She says the words quickly as well. As though she's afraid I'd mistake her questioning my drink for being unhappy with her own.

"No ice in mine. You like it?" I ask her, nodding to the drink in her hand and she nods back, biting down on her lip.

"Good."

I watch as her breathing comes in harder. I let my left hand fall to her thigh and then slip slowly down, trailing my fingers across her soft skin before gripping the edge of the barstool she's sitting on. Even with her up this high, I still tower over her. She's a petite little thing.

"You come on strong," she says, peeking up at me through her thick lashes. "Do you know that?"

I nod my head once and search her face for her reaction. "I don't do small talk," I tell her, thinking that's what she wants to hear.

"What if I want small talk?" she asks me without any trace of humor in her voice.

I make a show of taking an exaggerated look out the back window and tell her with a smile, "The weather's nice tonight."

She laughs at my stupid joke and the tension eases. Taking a step back, I pull out the barstool next to her further and take a seat.

"It's hard to get a read on you," I tell her and take another sip of the whiskey. It warms my chest as it goes down. It's the good stuff, not that cheap shit I have back at my place.

"Mm-hmm, I'm such a puzzle," she says flatly although I think it's meant to be taken with humor. There's something else there, some hint of truth that keeps me from laughing.

"Where are you from?" I ask her, keeping that small talk suggestion of hers in mind. I thought she'd be a bit easier than this. I know she wants it. And she knows I do too.

"Brunswick," she says, holding my gaze.

"Small world; I've got family in Brunswick," I tell her and start to think about my mother and the last time I was there. I regret referring to her as family the moment the word is out of my mouth. With both hands on my drink, I try to think of something else to talk about. The beer's already hitting me though, clouding my mind with memories I don't want to relive. Thankfully, she changes the subject.

"So, whose place is this?" she asks me and I tilt my head in James's direction, back by the arcade games. "His father's."

Spoiled rich kid is a term I'd use to describe James. I don't really like him. Then again, I don't much like anyone.

"Lot of alumni here," she says beneath her breath, glancing at the row of photographs on the walls rather than at James.

"Your family go here?" I ask her and she shakes her head. The only people I know who are here because it's their family's college are Kev and James. My family sure as shit didn't go to college.

"You're good at small talk," she says sweetly. "Maybe you should lead with that next time."

"Next time?" I ask her, cocking a brow and leaning forward.

"Yeah, next time, with the next girl you try to pick up," she says, and her legs swing slightly from side to side like she's getting a kick out of teasing me.

"You should know better than that," I tell her.

"Oh? Is this your last time?" She leans forward slightly. "You're done with your old ways and I'm the only one for you?" she says, mocking me.

"As in, you should know better than to think I'm giving up on chasing you until I get what I want," I correct her and hold her gaze. She breaks it though, easing back against the wall and crossing her ankles as she watches the pool game. The hard spheres crashing against one another and the crowd's reaction when one sinks makes me turn around for a moment.

"I like the chase," she says and then reaches out to brush her knuckles against my arm. "I bet you could catch me fast if I let you."

I huff a laugh and smirk at her. "If you let me?"

"Yeah," she says with a note of temptation in her voice like she's baiting me, then takes another drink.

"Allie Cat, you don't fool me. You love this little cat and mouse game."

"If I'm the cat, that means you're the mouse?" she asks me and it's only then that I realize what I said and how I said it. Maybe the whiskey's already getting to me.

"No, no, you got that wrong. You're my Allie Cat, but this game we're playing, I'm the one who's doing the chasing."

"Are you now?" she says in a seductive voice as she raises the cup to her lips. I don't know if it's the alcohol buzzing through my veins or the way she says it that makes me second-guess myself. She lets out a feminine chuckle into her cup and smiles at me with the hint of a blush creeping up her cheeks.

"I'm just playing with you, Dean," she says sweetly and slides off the barstool. I widen my legs as she stands between them and pops up on her tiptoes to plant a small kiss on the side of my jaw. I close my eyes, enjoying the soft touch. My fingers slide down the curve of her waist. But she pulls away before I can get more of what I want.

Just as she does, I see Kev and Brant make their way into the room. Allie brushes her fingers along my knuckles and then takes a step back, rocking on her heels.

"You're cute, but I have to go," she says and tugs her

hands away.

"Already?" I say. She hasn't even been here for an hour.

"I got shit to do," she tells me and I immediately bite back, "Yeah, me."

She gets a laugh out of that, spearing her fingers through her hair and the floral fragrance of her shampoo drifts toward me as she turns on her heels. "I'll see you on Monday," she murmurs innocently like I'm just going to watch her go.

"I can at least walk you out," I offer and stand up, reaching forward to snatch her by her waist.

She lets out a yelp that gets the attention of a few of the guys.

"I think I'm fine," she tells me and grabs my wrist, moving my hand off her waist.

A crease settles deep in my forehead and I can feel it when I say, "You don't want me to even walk you out?" I ask the question, but already I'm talking to her back.

She turns around to walk backward, teasing me some more. As she shakes her head, her hair falls over her shoulders, covering up that soft skin of hers. "Not tonight, Dean," she says.

"I don't know if this is a test, but that's bullshit if it is," I call after her, my feet planted firmly on the floor. Her sweet laugh follows her out of the room and I stay put.

I'll chase her if she wants, but fuck if I know what's going through that girl's mind.

Craziest thing though is that watching her leave only makes me want her more.

Chapter 11

Allison

My pen scribbles over the numbers, morphing them from identifiable figures to squares of black. I can't pay attention to the lecture, not when I can feel Dean's eyes on me.

I can hardly breathe as I close my eyes. I'm so close to the edge, to losing it and falling into a bottomless pit with no way to return. I can feel it now, how liberating it would be to just let go. Years of holding it in, years of doing nothing.

My eyes slowly open to the droning white noise of the professor's lecture. It's only then that I see I've broken the tip of the pen, the ink seeping into the pages and staining them.

Not just a few sheets but nearly all of them, maybe thirty or forty pages in this notepad. Have I been sitting here that long?

"You okay?" the girl to my right asks. I recognize her face. She has a certain look about her, like someone you could easily trust. Her voice is gentle too. She glances straight ahead and then back at me when I don't answer, merely staring at her and trying to snap out of it.

"Fine." I manage to push out the single word.

"I'm Angie, by the way," the girl whispers as she brushes her curly blond hair away from her face. Then she asks, "Do you need another pen?" She practically mouths the words so she doesn't disrupt the lecture.

"Oh, no," I say and wave her off, pushing away all the thoughts. "I'm fine, thanks."

We share an easy smile like nothing's happened. I suppose outwardly, nothing has. Just a broken pen and spilled ink on a notebook.

I hear a desk somewhere to the left of and behind me scratch across the floor. *Dean.* My body begs me to look back, but I don't.

God, I want to. It's different with him. A good different in some ways, but so bad in others.

He's a distraction.

With clammy hands, I reach into my bag and pull out another pen. I rip off a single piece of paper and wrap up the ruined pen, setting it to the side of the desk to toss on the way out.

That scraping sound catches my attention again, but this

time Angie's as well. She looks over her shoulder and then back to the front of the room.

My neck is refuses to budge, all because I can feel his gaze. I know he's watching and he's going to want an answer. Or an explanation. Or maybe neither. Maybe if I just ignore him, he'll leave me alone.

That's what I should want, but it hurts to think of that possibility. Inexplicably so.

It's funny how time passed so slowly before I came here. Every day was agonizingly painful. Now that I'm so very aware I need to make a decision, the class is over before I can let out a breath.

I need to force my body to relax and move normally so I'll look just like everyone else. The moment I do, I look behind me, arching my neck and succumbing to temptation.

Dean's dark eyes stare back at me.

I don't know how I thought for even one second he'd have looked away.

Maybe he has an obsession like I do.

All that anxiety, that fear, it all slips away as the clock ticks and our gazes meet. As though I'm his reflection, his lips lift into a slow smile and mine follow.

Dean could be my personal heroin. And I want a hit. I want it hard and fast.

It terrifies me. But I want that distraction more than ever now. I want him to take me away from this. However he can.

I know it'd be simple too. As effortless as jotting down on paper that I want him and exactly where to find me. It would be all too easy.

Time resumes as I wrap my hand around the leaking pen and toss it into the wastebasket at the front of the room. I don't look up as everyone walks past me heading for the exit, including Angie and her friendly smile. Trying to keep my composure, I head back to my seat, only to peek up and see Dean waiting for me.

I fucking love it. I love how he makes his intentions clear and that he's willing to give chase, to put himself out there. *I love that he wants me.*

"What's on your mind?" he asks me. My first instinct is to joke, to flirt, to keep things light.

If only he knew the truth.

He's already too close. And I'm too invested.

I should have stopped this before it got this far. A dark and deadly voice in the back of my mind whispers, coaxing in its cadence, *It has to happen. It's meant to be this way.*

"Nothing," I answer him immediately, ignoring the voice and reaching down for my bag.

"I knew it," he says with a cocky grin. "I knew there was literally nothing going on in there."

"Fucking asshole," I mutter as my smile broadens. I feel naturally at ease around him ... happy even. And that's dangerous. His rough chuckle makes my entire body heat.

Some places more than others.

"I can tell you what I was thinking," he says as he leans closer, so close that I get a hint of his cologne. It's clean and crisp, but with a hint of woodsy musk that makes me lean in too.

"I bet I already know exactly what you were thinking," I immediately retort, which only makes him scratch the stubble on his jaw, his smile ever present.

"What do you think?" he asks me, and I arch a brow to admonish him.

"Thoughts like that don't belong in the classroom."

"Where else are we going to find a desk?" he asks me, and I can't help how my thighs clench and my chest and cheeks warm with a slow, heated blush.

I always have a comeback but not this time.

"So, you want to go out?"

"No." I laugh off his suggestion. "Do *you* want to go out?"

"I could go out," he answers effortlessly. Like it doesn't bother him in the least.

"I don't know," I tell him, feeling that unease from earlier crawling back into my skin. I forget why I'm really here when I'm with him and I can't let that happen.

"You want a boyfriend or something?" Dean asks me, and I scoff. "What?" he says. "I don't know what the hell you want."

"Neither do I." I answer him with the most honesty I've spoken since I laid eyes on him and turn my back to leave.

"The hell you don't. You said you wanted me," he persists.

There's a certain tone in his voice and a flicker of something in his eyes that I recognize. It's a pain I know all too well. I hate it. I want to take it away and with Dean it'd be easy. He wants me, and I want him. There's so much more at stake, though.

A slow prickle of ice settles along my skin as I think about what's going to happen. I shouldn't lead him on like this. It's wrong.

But I've been fucked up for a while now, and he's just so tempting.

"You know I do," I tell him, turning around to face him after zipping up my bookbag. My lower back grazes it as my ass hits the desk. "I'd love for you to fuck me raw. Right here on this desk." I reach behind me to grip it and then nod my head to the side and add, "Or against the wall maybe."

His expression darkens with lust. I watch as his eyes widen with amusement at first, but even so, his pupils dilate with desire. Every second of silence is another degree of heat added between us.

I lean closer to him, feeling the tension rise as he adjusts his cock in his pants. His eyes don't move from my lips as I whisper, "I imagine it all the time." My fingertips play at the buttons on his shirt. Seeking consent, all the while luring him in.

"I bet you do too," I tell him, staring into his dark eyes and willing him to picture exactly what I've been dreaming about. "It would be bad for me, though. You'll fuck me then leave." At the last thought, my hands fall to my side. That's not the reason why, but I'm not above using the logic to keep him away.

It takes him a moment to process my confession. Like he's paralyzed from what I've done to him, and that gives me a thrill I can't put into words.

"So you do want a boyfriend?" he manages to say, and I'm equal parts amused and exasperated. The lies make the hole I'm digging for myself that much deeper.

"Look, Dean." I start to tell him it's not going to happen. I swear I had every intention of cutting him off. But there's a look in his eyes that makes my heart still just a beat too long. A look that heats the small space between us. A look that I'm addicted to.

"Yeah? I'm listening," Dean says as he takes a half step closer, decreasing the distance between us. He towers over me, his broad shoulders blocking out everything else. I'm caught in his gaze, caught in the moment.

I'll blame it all on that.

"If you want to fuck me, you should just show up at my house," I tell him and slip the ripped piece of paper in his hand.

The paper I've been scribbling on all class long.

The paper with my address on it.

Chapter 12

Dean

I don't know how I wound up outside of Allie's house with that scrap of paper in my pocket. It's part of a cute little row of houses off the edge of campus with white picket fences and a one-way street.

The only excuse I've got for showing up the moment my last class was over, is that I didn't have any blood my brain could use. It's all in my dick and that's the reason I ended up here, pushing the doorbell and acting like a damn puppy.

She said jump and I fucking jumped. But it's for pussy, so I can't beat myself up too much.

I shrug my shoulders to readjust my jacket as the sound of her walking through the house greets me from the other side of the door. There's a sheer curtain on the window and Allie pulls it back to look at me.

I only get a glimpse, but the look of surprise is something that makes me rethink what the hell I'm doing.

Until the door unlocks with a loud click and Allie opens it wide.

Any thoughts of turning around vanish. Her blouse hangs low and nearly covers up the cutoff jean shorts. It's thin and almost transparent, a button-down white number that would look professional with slacks.

But in those shorts and a burgundy bra, it's downright sinful.

"Dean," she says my name and then leans into the door, showing off the curve of her waist as she juts out her hip. "I wasn't expecting you, to be honest."

"I wasn't sure I was going to come either, but I thought you might want some company," I tell her and readjust my dick in my jeans. She knows what I want, and I have no intention of hiding it.

I love how she blushes just slightly, moving a finger to her lower lip as she gives me this shy smile that doesn't seem right on my Allie Cat.

"I guess I could use some," she says and moves aside to let me in, although the way she eyes me is more like a hunter and not the prey. Like she's the one in control here.

She needs a little lesson.

"I want your mouth first," I tell her as she closes the door.

She's quiet as she turns around, not answering me as I let my jacket slide off my shoulders and lay it on the back of a dining room chair.

The first floor of her place is small; a set of stairs to my left, an eat-in kitchen on the right and a cozy living room with a sofa. Right in front of us are a love seat and a TV stand. The sunshine filtering through the open blinds of her sliding doors is the only light in the place. I take a quick look around, wondering what she was up to before I came in, but she distracts me, letting out a small hum of appreciation.

"Is that so?" she asks, and I don't answer her. There's a teasing lilt in her voice that drives me crazy. It's a hint that she can take more. It suggests I'm not a man who can handle her.

What's more? She's letting me get away with pushing her. And I fucking love it. It only makes me want to push her harder.

She follows me in and her eyes roam down my body as I take off my shirt, tossing it on top of my jacket. I keep walking, moving to the window to shut the blinds and darkening the small living room. I want the lights on, though. I need to see this. Every. Fucking. Bit. of it.

"Yeah, mouth and then your cunt," I tell her confidently, flicking on a light switch and watching how she stalks toward me, those wide hips rocking back and forth and taunting me. My dick gets harder just watching her.

"You going to keep teasing me, Allie Cat?" I love how her breathing is coming out harder. A smirk kicks up my lips and then I lick them, slowly. Her eyes follow my movement and a shiver runs down her body. "I know you will. You love teasing me," I tell her with confidence and her gaze meets mine, narrowing as she decides what she wants to admit.

"Is that so?" she asks me in a flirtatious voice and takes a step back as I take one forward. The half smile widens.

"No more," I say and keep my tone stern. "You can tease me again tomorrow, but right now I'm done playing." My heart hammers hard in my chest, knowing how aggressive I'm being. But Allie's a woman who wants to be pushed.

"Tell me you don't want me right now," I offer her. "Tell me you don't want me to sink deep into you and fuck you how you deserve to be fucked, and I'll leave."

My heart spasms, hating that I've given her an out. But getting her enthusiastic consent first is key. I'm not really worried that she'll make me leave, though. I know Allie; I know what she wants, and I can give it to her better than any other man.

"I'm not a liar, Dean," she says quietly, and I watch as she catches her bottom lip between her teeth. "Yeah, I do."

"Say it."

"I want you. I want every inch of you."

"Good," I say and start to lean forward, to kiss those plump lips of hers, but she surprises me, dropping to her knees.

She doesn't say anything as she unzips my pants and I let her lead for now.

A little give, and a little take.

Her small hands pull my jeans down in a single tug and my thick cock juts out right in front of her face. A small gasp slips from her lips and I love how her eyes widen. I stroke my dick once, rubbing the precum already leaking out over the head.

Before I can take away my hand, she gives the head a quick lick, her tongue slipping along the slit and making me hiss.

Her eyes flash to mine as she wraps her lips around the head of my cock and sucks.

I don't hold back the groan from deep in the back of my throat. She deserves to know just how good she makes me feel. My hands fist her hair as she sucks me down, hollowing her cheeks and working my dick like a pro.

It's mesmerizing to watch her worshipping my cock with that sassy mouth of hers. I've thought about it every fucking night since I first saw her.

About time I have her right where I want her. I try to ignore the thoughts running through my head. The ones telling me this is a one-time thing. I already know I want more, and I refuse to let her deny me when this is through.

She moans around my cock and it sends a tingle up my spine. Fuck, she's even better than I thought she'd be.

I let her have her fun for a minute and then I shove myself to the back of her throat. Again, and again, and again. "Fuck," I groan. My blunt nails dig into the back of her head as my toes curl and my eyes shut tight. She feels too fucking good. "I'm going to cum just from your mouth," I barely get out through my clenched teeth.

She continues like she didn't hear me, swallowing me down and trying to take more of my length. I have to pull out before I lose it. I'm not ready to be done just yet. My breath leaves me as she pants, quickly trying to catch her breath. I stare down at her and I'm in awe of her eagerness for more. Her lips are swollen and her eyes wide and glassy.

She's fucking perfect. A greedy little slut just for me.

She opens her mouth wider and leans forward as I stroke my cock once, running my palm over the head. The air is chilly compared to her hot mouth, but I can't let her suck me off anymore. If I do, it'll all be over too soon. I didn't come here for a blowjob. I want more from her.

"Get up," I tell her sternly as if she doesn't have me on the edge of coming undone. She reacts immediately, desperate to please me and I can't help but notice how her upper thighs clench and she whimpers softly.

I'm not careful as I rip open her shirt, forcing a button to pop off and fall to the floor. Her gasp reminds me to keep a straight face. *I'm in control*, I tell myself as I unclasp her bra. It dangles in front of her, laying across her torso as the straps are caught in her sleeves. But her full breasts stand at attention, her pale pink nipples pebbling and making my mouth water. She stands like a mannequin, letting me almost violently undress her.

My dick twitches when I run the back of my hands across

her hardened peaks. My tongue grazes across my lower lip before I dip down and take her left breast into my mouth. Sucking and swirling my tongue around her sensitive bud.

She reacts exactly how I want, spearing her hands through my hair and arching her back. Her soft, strangled moans of pleasure are music to my ears.

I release her nipple from my mouth with a loud pop and take my time playing with the other one, pinching it between my thumb and forefinger before sucking it into my mouth. I bite down just slightly, and she hisses. Not holding back my smile with my teeth still clamped, I pull back again and watch her face as I do. Her eyes are wide, and her mouth forms a perfect O. The same mouth that just sucked me off like that's what it was made to do.

When I release her, I take a step back and I miss her instantly. Her breathing is shallow as her hands move to the button on her shorts but she hesitates, waiting for me to give her permission.

I let her stand there, looking at me and dying for her own release as I stroke myself. The sight of her is everything to me. I want a fucking photograph so I can remember this moment forever.

Her hair already looks like she's just been fucked. Her green eyes are dark with desire, and with a torn shirt and her gorgeous breasts bared, she's everything I've ever wanted.

"I don't know if I want the shirt on while I fuck you or

not," I say out loud although it's more of a thought and not a question. More of a tease for her than anything else.

She shifts her weight and stands there patiently, waiting for my decision. I stroke my dick again and her eyes instantly dart down to watch. Still, she's quiet. Good girl.

"Take it off, all of it, and bend over," I tell her and nod to the armrest of the sofa. She obeys but undresses slowly, letting each garment fall to the floor as I step out of my jeans.

The second I slip inside of her, I know I'm fucked.

I'll need more than tonight. *More of her.* She feels too fucking good.

I'm not gentle with her. I love how her face presses into the cushion. How she doesn't hold back the screams as I pound into her all the way to the hilt on the first stroke.

The sounds of wet flesh smacking together mixed with her cries of want make me fuck her harder. My balls slam against her clit over and over as I push into her as deep as I can with each thrust.

Her nails scratch on the fabric as she screams out my name and it's all I can take.

Her pussy spasms and I empty myself inside of her.

I can't breathe as I collapse on top of her, bracing my weight with my forearms and kissing her upper back and shoulders with soft, open-mouth kisses that make her shudder again.

I let the tip of my nose glide along her back, smelling her sweet scent as I give her one last kiss.

After I catch my breath, still buried inside of her I say, "I told you that you wanted me."

She tosses her hair over her shoulder to look back at me, her ass still up and my cum leaking from her pretty pink pussy. A soft moan leaves her, making her chest rise and fall before she replies, "Pretty sure you're the one who was dying for this, Dean."

Chapter 13

Allison

One-night stands are easy.

I come, and I go. I smirk at the thought. They make me feel better for a while and then when I want more, I find someone else. I'm safe and always use protection; everything always happens on my terms too. It's always easy that way.

But *he* isn't a one-night stand. He's not one of the guys I'd go pick up at the back of O'Malley's. A man whose face I'd never see again. I've had my share. I've wasted so many nights waiting to be taken back to a shitty motel or fucked against the side of a car.

I loved each and every one. Because they made me feel better in some fucked-up way.

I always knew I could leave them behind me and walk away like nothing had happened.

Dean will be right in my path after tonight. I can't get away from him. I can't say goodbye and never see him again. Worse, I let it happen.

I should have known better than to have Dean come here. It's a rule: never at my place. I don't break my rules. Never. My back teeth grind as I remember my slipup. Well, two of them. I didn't even make him wear a rubber. The thought should anger me but instead it makes me feel deliciously dirty. I let myself get carried away. I should have thought it out more. I shouldn't be so damn reckless.

The bathroom light switches off and he appears in all his glory in the doorway. Stark naked with chiseled abs and his thick cock still at half-mast.

I can see why he's so fucking conceited now.

He lazily scratches the back of his head as he stalks toward me, not at all trying to cover up any part of his body. I've slipped my shorts back on already and I'm busy pulling up a bra strap when he asks, "What are you doing?"

"What's it look like?" I answer him with a side-eye and bend down to pick up my shirt. Which is torn beyond any hope of repair. The memory makes my pussy clench and the sweet ache only makes me want Dean again. "Well, I guess this is trash now," I say although it comes out light and humorous more than anything else.

I can feel how my body reacts to his. It's innate. It's clear from the way I peek at him through my lashes, the way the heat creeps up into my cheeks and even how my breathing is attuned to his.

Like prey to a hunter ... or vice versa.

With him, it's dangerous because I desperately want to be the prey.

His face scrunches in sympathy. "Sorry about that," he says, taking the shirt from my hands and letting his strong fingers brush against mine. They're rough to the touch and send sparks of want through me, even as the soreness between my thighs intensifies by the second. Dean's damn good at what he does. I'll give him that.

"You want me to get you a new one?" he asks me.

"Why? So you can rip that one up too?"

"What else am I good for?" he jokes as I shake my head and stare at the ruined fabric in my hands.

"I knew you were bad news," I say and again it's meant as a tease, to come out playfully and add to the banter between us.

"You don't know my story," he says and his voice comes out hard. No humor, only defensiveness.

I'm caught off guard as I watch him bend down for his shirt. Still completely naked, but he reaches for the shirt first, of all things.

"Really?" I tease him, pretending the tension doesn't exist. I wait for him to look up at me and that guarded expression still clouds his handsome face. It calls to me differently than before. My fingers itch to touch his jaw. To calm the sadness, but I resist. "Your shirt is what you go for first?" I keep my voice light and he huffs out a breath but lets a smile grow on his face.

"It's for you," he tells me as he balls it up and hands it to me. "Since you're so hell-bent on having me rip another shirt off you."

The laughter that erupts from me at his response is genuine, as is the warmth that flows through me. He's bad news *for me*. He doesn't get that. It's all bad news waiting to happen.

"It's been a while since I've smiled this hard," I confess and then bite back the happiness and honesty in that statement.

"That's a shame," Dean says and takes the shirt back before I can accept it. "You've got a beautiful smile." He leaves it hanging there in the air, and I take the bait, reaching out and trying to snatch it from him. A rough chuckle fills the air between us when I miss.

"You want it?" he asks me with a smirk on his face.

Do I want his shirt? I'm in my own damn house. I could go upstairs and put on whatever I want. But do I want his? The one he's taunting me with? Not to mention the only shirt he has here.

I nod once, feeling my hair tickle my back. The stare between us grows hotter as he takes a half step back, but holds out the shirt. My heart races faster with each passing second and the tips of my fingers glide against one another as he shakes it, as if to say, "Here, it's all yours."

I act as fast as I can, reaching for it and tearing it from him, but it's in vain.

He lets me have it without a fight in the least.

The cotton shirt is bunched in my hands as he drops his to his side and scratches his abs.

"Aw, you're even prettier when you pout," he mocks me and I roll my eyes, tossing his shirt carelessly behind him.

"You're no fun," I tell him. He takes a large stride toward me, wrapping his arms around my waist and pulling me against his hard chest before I can blink.

"Allie Cat, all you have to do is tell me you want it," he says as I gasp and reach both my hands up to his bare chest. My blood heats as he lowers his lips to the shell of my ear. "Sometimes it's fun to take, but we both know how that would end between us," he whispers, and it sends a chill across my skin.

He nips at my neck and runs the tip of his nose along my jaw. My eyes close slowly as I lift my lips to his. The first kiss is gradual, teasing even; I'm still reeling from his comment. The second is deeper but the moment his tongue slips across the seam of my lips, I have to laugh. His dick is hard again and poking me in my stomach.

I pull away from him, but just with my upper half, seeing as how he still has a firm grip on my waist.

"Already wanting more?" I tease him. He groans deep and presses another kiss to my lips. This time I open my mouth, greeting his hot tongue with swift, deep strokes of my own.

I moan into his mouth as he slowly unbuttons my shorts and yanks them down, shoving his hands between my legs and cupping between my thighs like he owns what's there. My neck arches and my strangled cry of pleasure is muted when Dean covers my mouth with his. He devours me forcefully and unapologetically.

And I can't bring myself to regret it.

Not this time or the next. Not even when I wake up early the next morning to find he's already gone but left his shirt behind with a note telling me it's mine to keep until he replaces the other.

At least he left a note. I'll give him that.

Chapter 14

Dean

My muscles ache, and the burn feels so fucking good. My heart's racing and I can faintly taste the blood from the cut on my lip.

I live for this shit.

My pops used to watch rugby. I don't have many fond memories of him since he was sick for so long but as I stand in my position, cracking each knuckle one by one and waiting for the signal, I remember how I used to sit cross-legged only inches from the screen when we'd watch television together. I can still smell the beer Pops always had next to him during a game. I can still hear him cheering them on. And the second I can, I rush forward, crashing my skull into Kev's shoulder and digging my hands between his chest and the ball.

My teeth are clenched; my heart isn't fucking moving. Nothing is.

All that matters is that I get possession. My shoulder knocks hard against Kev's and he's thrown backward. As I fall forward, I rip the ball out of his hands and quickly throw it to Daniel. Fast possession, fast plays.

I tumble downward and don't even try to brace myself. My shoulder cracks as it meets the ground and the wind is knocked from me.

Before I can even get up, Kev's shoving me back down to the ground, nearly trampling me to get to the action. Fucker steps on my hand, grinding it into the dirt. Fuck!

My eyes narrow as my breath comes back to me. I almost grab his ankle and yank it toward me, just to see his scrawny ass bust his mouth on the way down. But I bite back the anger. It's not what I need. It's not good for me.

A whistle goes off and Brant, the third player on our side, pats my back as I stand up, brushing the soil from a scratch on my arm. His hand thumps my back as he says something I can't make out over the ringing in my ears. I focus on counting in my head.

Counting all the times I've lost control. All the times I've let my anger get the better of me.

All the shit it's brought me. Several broken noses, although I've only had one myself. It's one thing to pop off and pick fights because I'm bored, or because I'm angry, or even because I'm fucking lost. It's another thing entirely to let it control me. To fall back on it. I know this, I've been over this shit with Dr. Robinson, but I'll be damned if it helps me as much as getting locked up did.

I can hear the guys rallying up again as the white noise and ringing slowly fades.

All I'm concentrating on is my rage, taming it. Keeping it in. After all, it's Kev's uncle who helped me out. He's friends with the judge who agreed to the terms of my probation and beating the shit out of his nephew isn't the best way to pay him back.

"Fuck yeah, man!" I hear Daniel yell in a deep voice before throwing the ball down on the ground in front of me and jumping on my side, wrapping his arms around my neck and thrusting his hips once before jumping off.

"Whoo!" he calls out, clearly pleased with himself and the team. The smile stretches slowly across my face as I watch as him celebrate with Brant.

"Go, team!" I hear her soft feminine voice shouting and cheering before I see her.

Hard to believe that sweet voice could come from such a sinful mouth. I can't help but to look over at her; Allie's in the back of the bleachers this time, clapping her hands and blending in with the small crowd. Well she's trying to, but a woman like that wasn't meant to blend in. It's not even so much a crowd as it is a group of kids killing time before class.

It doesn't look like any of them are paying attention.

She smiles brightly when I catch her gaze. I wasn't sure if I'd see her today or not. Everything I did yesterday morning was deliberate.

Leaving my shirt—it was an excuse to seek her out in case she doesn't come back to me.

Not leaving my number—so she can't snub me and leave me hanging. I got her number from her phone before leaving, though. I didn't say I play fair.

And taking off before she woke up—to make her want the chase this time.

Yesterday came and went easily enough. I thought about her ass and almost texted her. I'd feel pathetic about how she's got me wrapped around her little finger if she wasn't sitting in the bleachers right now.

She came because she wants to see me. Plain and simple.

And I fucking love that.

My little Allie Cat may think that was a one-time thing, but I'm not even close to having my fill yet. She's a girl I can play with and I can already feel the excitement in my blood at what I'm going to do to her.

"Lookee, lookee," I hear Kevin say as we huddle up. When I look to my left at him, his eyes are on her. "You got yourself a fan, bro," he tells me and wraps his arm around me. Today we're on opposite sides, mixing it up for fun.

"Let's run some more fast plays," James starts saying,

hands on his knees and far too into practice. As if anyone really cares about this game.

"You tap that?" Kev asks and it irritates James, but only for a second, until he looks behind my shoulder and catches sight of her.

Daniel peeks up at her too.

"What the fuck?" I snap at them.

"I was just looking," Daniel says defensively and tilts up his chin and adds, "Didn't take long, huh?"

"Longer than I wanted," I tell them and it makes Kev's brows knit together. "She likes to be chased," I explain and then feel uncomfortable talking about her to these guys. I barely fucking know them and it's none of their business.

They don't need to know that she's a challenge. Because she's for me. Not them.

"Let's just call it," Brant says. "Sun's going down and I'm fucking beat."

"Nah, one more," James argues. "We're getting lazy as fuck."

I crack my neck to one side and then the other.

"So, what's she like?" Kev asks, nudging me and yet again pulling the topic back to Allie.

"Fucking worth it," I tell him without hesitation. I knew she'd feel like that. Tight in all the right places, gripping my dick and working it like it belonged to her. There's more to come. I can already taste it. There's something in her that's just like me. Something easy to recognize. I can feel it. And I know it's going to make it that much better when I have her next.

"She likes it rough, doesn't she?" Kev asks and James elbows him as he adds, "Rough and dirty."

I catch Daniel glancing between the two of us. He doesn't say anything, but I don't like the look on his face or the shit they're saying.

"We going in again or not?" Kev asks. I couldn't give two shits.

"Once more," Daniel finally speaks up. Then he asks, "You want the goal this time? Chicks fucking love it when you score." I snort at his suggestion.

"Yeah they do," Brant agrees with him and again he looks back to check her out.

I shrug like I don't give a damn but then say, "Yeah, I want it this time."

"Yeah you want it," James says like a jackass. He humps the air like a jackass too. I rub the back of my head, feeling my ears burn.

"Fucking embarrassing," Daniel says, pushing James over so he falls on his ass. As the other guys laugh, I look behind me, just a quick glance to see if she saw.

But I don't know if she did or not, because she's already gone.

Chapter 15

Allison

He keeps looking over at the bleachers like I'm going to magically appear, and I can't help that it makes me smile. But the tug upward on my lips falters as quickly as it forms.

I know this story. And the sweet bubbly feelings in my chest, well, they don't mean shit compared to the growing sense of dread in the pit in my stomach.

I'm smarter than this.

But I want him.

The smile widens, and I kick up my foot to hit the brick wall behind me when the guys walk this way. Straight to the locker room I just happen to be standing in front of.

It gives me a sick sense of pleasure when Dean nearly

trips as he catches sight of me.

He notices my smile too, which makes him narrow his eyes. I love this game. More than anything else, I love the way it makes me feel.

Even if it is temporary.

"Stay right there," Dean tells me, not slowing his pace as he walks right past me to go through the doors. "Just need to grab something."

He doesn't even wait for me to nod. Doesn't wait for any sign at all I heard him.

My jaw hangs open. Fucking dick.

I grin slightly as I realize he won that round. I can hear a bell ding in my head and see him getting a point on a scoreboard. "Touché," I mutter as the rest of the guys file in. He knows I came for him.

Why do I love that he's such an asshole?

I'm left pondering that very question and kicking the dirt when I hear another voice.

"Well, hello again. Did you enjoy the game?" Kevin Henderson asks me as the hairs on the back of my neck stand up. He stops only a foot in front of me, watching as some of the other guys walk past him. I have to remind myself we're not alone. Not really. The field is right behind us. The study group that was on the bleachers is still there. Still within earshot.

My shoulders move involuntarily into a shrug as I try to act casual and keep it light, but flirtatious. It takes me a moment to look Kevin in the eyes and when I do, I make sure to flash him a dazzling smile.

"Looked like a practice to me," I tell him while my heart thuds once, then twice. *It's not a game.*

He manages a half smirk and moves his thumb to the corner of his mouth before replying, "I thought you said it's always a game?"

The pounding of my heart gets louder and my blood turns to ice in my veins. I can picture how it would happen right now, how he'd pin me here against the brick wall, how it would scrape against my back. But it would have to be late. The skies would be black and my scream, when I finally did scream, would echo for miles.

"Didn't you?" he asks me, his voice bringing me back to the present and I have to manage my composure, making sure I add a touch of shyness as I take the strand of hair in front of my face and tuck it behind my ear.

My eyelashes flutter as I tell him, "You have a good memory."

"You dye your hair?" he asks and my stomach clenches. As if he knows who I used to be. "Why? Blondes have more fun, don't they?" he says in jest before flashing me a smile and I struggle to respond. *He's just making random conversation. It doesn't mean anything.*

"Yo," Kevin says as he rips his eyes off me and the sound of footsteps slowly coming to a stop greet me.

"Everything good?" I hear Dean ask, but I still don't look in his direction. I can't right now. Not after this little encounter.

It's odd to feel as if I've betrayed him. As if I should feel guilty, and maybe that's what this twisting in my gut is.

"Yeah, yeah," Kevin says and tells me, "Catch you later," before half jogging into the locker room.

"He giving you a hard time?" Dean asks me and when I hear Kevin's sneakers skid across the cement pad in front of the doorway, I finally look up at Dean. Right into a possessive stare.

One that sees right through me.

His hard gaze makes me feel like my hand has been played. Like I can't trust the words in my mouth.

"You want to tell me something?" he asks me and my bottom lip wobbles slightly. I want to tell him everything. *I'm desperate to tell someone.*

"Did you see him score?" Daniel's voice interjects. When I look at him, Dean takes a step back, narrowing his eyes and focusing them on Daniel. "He said it was for you," Daniel adds as he slips his arm around Dean's shoulders and flashes me a charming smile, but I see right through it.

He's a good liar. From what I've heard in the last few weeks from whispers on campus, it's a family trait of his. Apparently all the Cross' have a reputation. I don't know what the hell Daniel Cross is doing here or with men like Kev and I don't care. Consequences be damned, I'm going to get what I want.

"I saw a bit of the action," I finally answer Daniel and then meet Dean's stare to add, "I like watching him score."

A flicker of humor touches his eyes but he doesn't smile until I say, "I'm glad you guys are done, though. I don't like waiting for what I want."

I shouldn't have said it really. But I wanted to see him smile. I wanted it so bad that I lost control again. He makes me reckless.

"You heard her," Dean says with a lopsided grin and slaps Daniel's arm away.

"You made her wait long enough I guess," Daniel says before walking off and nodding a farewell.

A short moment passes and I don't know what Dean's next move will be. It makes me nervous.

"So, you ready to go?" Dean asks me, and I gawk at him.

"Go where?"

The muscles on his broad shoulders ripple as he moves the strap of his duffle bag over his shoulder and across his body.

"I just came to give you your shirt back."

"That's nice of you," he says then looks at my purse and my cheeks burn. I don't actually have it with me. I just said that to make it difficult for him.

"So?" he asks and another breeze goes by, sending goosebumps up my arm. It's colder in the evening and especially in the shadows.

"So what?"

"The shirt?" he asks then adds, "Really, it's for you to hold on to until I can get you a new one."

I shrug off the chill. "You don't have to do that."

"I want to, though. You all right with that?" he asks like it's a dare and my heart skips a beat as I'm caught in his heated gaze. He traps me so easily.

Luckily, I'm saved by his next comment.

"I like being with you for some reason." It's a backhanded compliment. He's such an asshole. But such a good-looking, playful one.

"Yeah, well, you're an asshole jock and jocks aren't my thing," I tell him back just as dismissively. Both of us are smiling, though. This is what I like about him.

"I'm not a jock."

I wait for him to comment on the asshole part and when he doesn't, I let out a small laugh.

Rolling my eyes, I wrap my arms around my chest as a gust blows my hair off my shoulder. Dean looks up and it's as if that's the cue for the sky to visibly darken.

"So, where do you want to go?" he asks.

"I'm not sure that's smart."

"It's just a date."

"I don't think we should date. I don't really do dating." My gaze falls to his chest, moves to his shoes then continues to the ground as I feel the truth of why I even bothered to go against my gut and show up to the field today. I push the hair back from my face as the breeze picks up and wish I'd worn a thicker coat.

The sound of Dean rustling in his duffle bag gets my

attention, and he pulls out a jacket then hands it out to me. "Put it on," he tells me and it's clearly a command. Like a good girl, I reach out for it, but then feel ridiculous and pathetic and drop my hand before I grab it.

"Dean, I'm not good for you." I push out the words even though they hurt, even though they make me feel worse than just playing along.

"You're cute, Allie Cat, but that 'it's not you, it's me' bullshit isn't going to work on me. I'm too used to being pushed away," he tells me, and I watch his expression shift as he realizes what he's said. He's used to being pushed away. I'd just be one more asshole doing the same.

"Come on, take it," he urges, shaking the jacket and the memory of last night forces me to take it.

I'm silent as I put it on. Fuck. Shit. Dammit. I hate this. I hate that I started this.

"So, date," Dean says as he grips the strap with both of his hands and watches me slip on his jacket. It's oddly warm for being so thin. "Where are we going?" he asks.

I roll my eyes and tell him, "I don't date."

"Just fucking then," he says, nodding his head. "Your place or mine?" he asks with a cocky grin.

"I'm not here just so you can get in my pants," I say, trying desperately to clear my head and figure out what the hell I'm doing.

"Then why'd you come?" he asks me.

"I told you I just wanted to give you your shirt back," I tell him, but I can already see the spark of mischievousness in his eyes.

"I was talking about the other night, and it's because you fucking loved it."

I can't help the smile that comes with his joke or the way his dirty words make me feel like it's all okay. Belting his chest, I turn away from him. "You're awful," is all I can say, the smile still there. When he slides up behind me, pulling my body close to his, I relax into his heat. I hear the wind blow behind us but with my back to his chest, and my body facing the wall, not a bit of it touches my skin. Instead of a chill, I'm greeted with warmth as he gently nips my jaw and then releases me.

"You look good in my clothes," he tells me when I turn to face him. His eyes roam freely down my body and the heat intensifies in my cheeks.

"Thanks for the jacket." It's only a quiet whisper but I mean it. I'm grateful for him.

Both of us are silent as we watch a few more guys leave the locker room. I cross my arms over my chest and peek up at him.

"I like you, Allison," Dean says, taking a step forward. "I'm not going to let you get away so easily."

My lungs still for a moment as his fingers brush along my face and he tucks a strand of hair behind my ear.

"Maybe I'd like that," I say, admitting the sentiment out

loud. The moment I do, I'm certain I shouldn't have said them.

"We're going to fuck, but I need to eat first," he tells me. "And you're coming with me because you need to eat too."

"You're taking me out to dinner?" I ask incredulously, although I'm not blind to the fact that it makes me happy. Truly. That should bother me more than it does. All of this should bother me much more than it does.

"Just feeding you, Allie Cat. Don't read too much into it."

"I thought we were just fucking?" I say.

"A man's got to eat."

I huff a response, although the smile lingers on my lips. But only for a moment.

Chapter 16

Dean

The corner diner on campus isn't classy or fancy. The booths are covered in red vinyl that matches the stools at the narrow bar in front of the kitchen. The black and white checkered floors, vinyl records on the wall and jukebox in the far corner give it a retro feel. It's not really what I'd consider a good date place but they make a damn good burger.

Allie takes the lead the second we walk in, heading for a booth at the back and I follow her. She's been quiet since we left the field, and I don't like it.

I don't like the way she was looking at Kev even more.

A waitress carrying two baskets of fries calls out, "Be right with you," as I take my seat in the booth Allie picked.

"You been here yet?" I ask Allie, still trying to figure out what's going on in her pretty little head.

She lifts a brow at me as she slips the jacket off her shoulders. *My* jacket. "You learn quick," she tells me, and I feel my forehead crease.

"How's that?"

"Small talk, you do well when you lead with it."

There's a hum of pleasure running through me when she smiles. "I try," I say and then glance over my shoulder as the waitress heads back to the kitchen rather than toward us.

When I look back at Allie, she's quiet again, a contemplative look on her face.

I can't help but wonder if it's because of Kevin. Maybe he's the one she really wanted.

My muscles coil at the thought and I can feel anger rising at the thought of her with him. *She's mine.* That little prick isn't good enough for her.

I pick at the napkin on the table out of habit, my mind going back to the sight of her batting her lashes at him and giving him that sweet look that belongs to me. Doesn't she know better than that? I'll treat her good. I have what it takes to keep her.

"So, you don't like jocks?" I ask, preparing to bring it up. To make sure she knows her ass is mine right now. Even in kindergarten, everyone knew it—I don't share well with others.

"Not really," she answers me, but that playfulness in her

voice is gone. She squirms in her seat like she's uncomfortable.

"They're just not your type?" I ask with my eyes narrowing, each second bringing me closer to the place I was when I came out of the locker room and saw her with him.

She meets my gaze head-on. "I've fucked a lot of them, but I guess I just prefer other types of guys."

"You like being thought of like that, don't you?"

"Like what?" she says, egging me on.

"Like a slut," I say, not missing a beat.

"I like it when people call me that to my face. I like them to know it doesn't bother me. I fucking own it." Her breathing picks up, her body tensing. Like she's ready for a fight and to defend her position. I don't want a fight, though. I fucking love how she knows what she wants.

"Then what type do you like? Since you're so good at owning it."

"I have lots of types, I guess."

"But no one type in particular?" I ask her. "Not like, I don't know, my height, my eye color?" She barely looks at me and then I add, "Tall, dark, and handsome?" I expect her to laugh or give me something back. But I get nothing.

Something happened between the time I walked into the locker and the time I came out. I'm damn sure of it because I've never seen her like this.

She presses her lips together in a thin line and looks past me when a loud bang and clatter comes from the kitchen.

The couple at the other end of the restaurant is looking too.

It's only when I look back to the piece of napkin in my hands that I realize it's shredded.

"No. No type in particular," Allie says flatly.

"You're being moody as fuck."

"I'm just moody in general," she says with a smile that doesn't reach her eyes. Those beautiful eyes are narrowed at me and I know she's warring with something, but I don't know what. I just want her to tell me.

"Give me something." The words may come out as a command but I'm fucking begging. I'm practically on my knees wanting this girl to trust me.

"Something?" That resolute look in her eyes flickers, like she didn't expect that. *Like she didn't expect me.*

"You don't have to hide from me," I start to say but before I can finish, she's already shaking her head.

"I didn't ask for this," she bites back.

"Then leave," I tell her because I'm irritated. Because the fact that she's giving me attitude and pushing me away is doing nothing but pissing me off.

It takes all of half a second for her to stand up, leaving my jacket where it is, and make a beeline for the back exit.

"What the hell is wrong with you?" I call after her.

"A lot," she answers, and I should let her walk away. I should watch her do it and order myself something to eat. Forget about her.

I'm sure there's a lot of shit I should do, but logic and reasoning aren't really my strong suit.

And I fucking want her.

More than anything else right now. I. Want. Her.

I shove the table away as I stand, and it squeaks across the floor. "Allison," I call after her as the door shuts, but she doesn't look back.

I'm quick. Quicker than her as I round the back exit to the deserted parking lot.

My hand slams on the brick wall as I catch up to her, boxing her in and stopping her in her tracks.

"You're in my way," she says through gritted teeth.

"I don't like games."

"I told you, Dean," she says sarcastically, although her expression is riddled with pain. "It's always a game."

"What's going on with you? You're making me crazy with this shit."

"You think I don't care about myself, huh? That I don't have any self-worth?"

"Where the fuck is that coming from?"

"From you asking me if I'm a slut."

"That's not what I said, I said you like being thought of like that. There's a difference."

Her expression softens slightly but she continues this bullshit. "It's the same for you."

"It's not. And I didn't say shit about your *self-worth*." I mock the way she said it and feel like an ass, but it pisses me off she'd even say that. "I only want you because you are worth it. How can you not see that?"

She flinches at my question.

"Just let me go," she whispers and pushes at my arm, but I hold firm.

"No, you're not leaving like this." I've never met someone like her. She needs someone. It's so fucking obvious.

"You don't get to tell me what to do," she says but even as she does, I can see her fight is gone.

We're in the back lot, with dumpsters right behind us and there are only two cars back here. We have plenty of privacy and at the realization, I step even closer to her. Upping the ante.

"You're not leaving like this. Not until you give me an explanation."

"Fuck you," she tells me.

"That's right, Allie Cat, that's exactly what you're about to do. You're finally getting fucked against the wall like the dirty whore you are."

"I already crossed that off my wish list."

"Not with me and not like this. And it's not your wish list, Allison, it's your to-do list."

"You're such a cocky bastard. You think because you tell me to fuck you, I will."

"No, it's because you want to. It's because you love it when my dick's deep inside of you. And I may be cocky, but you're the one who's pushy. You want control, you want to pull me this way and that and the moment I follow, you want to push me away. Not. Fucking. Happening."

"You think you're so good, don't you?" she taunts me.

"Tell me I'm not, and I'll leave."

My heart's a fucking battering ram, trying to crash out of my chest, but she doesn't answer me. She bites tongue for once.

I know one thing about Allie. She'll stay with me if I'm loving on her. I can do that. I can keep her coming back.

"Now, getting back to your to-do list. You're going to take my cock into your tight cunt that's already wet for me. Then you're going back inside and you're going to sit down next to me while my cum leaks out of your cunt like the dirty girl you are."

"Just because I liked it once, doesn't mean I'll like it again," she tells me and shoves against my chest. The look on her face tells me everything I need to know.

She wants to hurt me. To push me away. I won't let it happen. I can't.

"I let a lot of people push me out of their lives. None of them wanted me. But you do. I know you do," I tell her, and I'm shocked by the admission. The look on her face shows she's surprised too.

"What are you doing to me?" I ask her although there's no way in hell she could answer.

The air changes in an instant and I feel weak. Like I've lost her, all because I can't control my mouth.

I pull my arm away, my palm stinging from being against the hard brick for so long. *What the fuck is she doing to me?*

"Can I tell you something, Dean?" she says and lowers her voice, her features softening. Half of me expects her to kiss me, the other half thinks she's going to slam her head into my nose. I never know what to expect from her.

"Tell me whatever you want, Allie."

"You scare me."

"I don't mean to," I tell her apologetically. My face falls. "Fuck, that's the last thing I want."

"No, no, not like that," she's quick to respond and this time she actually comes to me.

"Like what, then? I can fix it." Damn, I sound like a little bitch. Even hearing it in my own voice, I don't care. Because she cups my jaw and leans in to say, "I feel like I'm safe when I'm with you, and that scares the fuck out of me." Her whisper gently caresses my jaw and a chill runs down my neck.

"Let's pretend that's a good thing," I tell her, and she gives me a sad smile.

"I don't do well with pretending."

"I don't believe that for a second. I bet you have lots of fantasies."

"That's not the same."

"Yeah it is," I say and cup her cheek in my hand. I press a kiss to her forehead and whisper, "I bet you'd like to pretend with me."

Her body shivers beneath me. A shiver that makes me feel like I've won.

"I like the idea of you ..." she trails off, closes her eyes and whispers, "pushing me against the wall." When she opens her eyes, it looks like she's not breathing. Her green eyes stare back at me with an unspoken question. Asking if I understand what she's saying.

"And then what?" I ask her as my mouth goes dry. The need to taste her, to shove her back and take from her is riding me hard. I have her right now, but I need to give her every reason to stay. My hands clench into fists at my side and my body goes rigid. One piece of my anatomy is noticeably harder than the rest.

"I'd like it," she barely speaks the words before visibly swallowing. "I'd like it if you were rough. If you ..." she trails off while her gaze falls away from mine and she takes an unsteady breath.

"You want me to fuck you like I own you. Like your cunt belongs to me and I'll take what I want from you?" I ask her and finally trust myself enough to take her small hand in mine. My touch is gentle as I rub the rough pad of my thumb along her knuckles.

"Yes," she answers me quickly and I take a half step back, so I can look her in the eyes, searching them and trying to decide if she knows what she's asking for.

"If I did what I wanted to you," I start to say and then

want to take it back. I can already see this going the wrong way. Back to her leaving me.

"What?" she asks.

I look at the empty parking lot and then back at her. *Give and take.* I gave some; I can take it now.

"What if I punished you?" I suggest as I run the back of my pointer finger down the side of her face. "For flirting with another man." I almost say one of my friends. *Kevin.* I almost single him out. But I have a feeling Allie likes to flirt a lot. And with whomever the fuck she wants.

I'd admire that if her ass wasn't already claimed by me.

She glares at me.

It's full of defiance and even a touch of hate. I can't take her hate. That's not what I want from her.

I almost take it back. I'm so close to apologizing but then she opens that mouth of hers.

"I can do what I want," she finally says. Her eyes dare me to contradict her.

"You already told me you wanted me, and that comes with a price," I tell her. "You know better than that, Allie."

"If I want attention, I'm going to get it," she speaks softly, staring past my shoulder and out across the parking lot. I can give that to her. Anything she needs, I can give to her.

"You just need to be fucked, don't you? You'd fall on anyone's dick to please this greedy little cunt."

Her lips part, but she hesitates.

"Fuck you," she finally says but it's half-hearted and she's breathing heavier. And that's just what I need. A sign that she still wants me. Or at least will give me a chance.

"That's exactly what I want," I tell her and she scoffs, but doesn't break the heated gaze between us.

I take a step forward and she takes one back, but it's shorter than mine, stopped by the hard brick wall behind her.

"Don't you know this is mine until I've had my fill?" I say beneath my breath as I reach between her thighs and cup her pussy.

Her mouth parts slightly, even as her back arches and she pushes her cunt against my hand.

"You're bad for me," she tells me in a heated whisper and then her eyes close with a small moan as I rock my palm against her clit.

I might not be the best thing for her, but that doesn't mean I'm letting her go.

I pull away right before those soft moans can turn into something more than just foreplay.

"Tell me what you want." I give her the command, but it comes out as desperate. One half step back gives her the exit she was after when I walked out here. "Just tell me, Allie."

I don't care that I'm weak for her. I just want her weak for me.

"I want you," she says in a rushed breath and before the last word is spoken, I'm already on her. Shoving my hands up her skirt and ripping my thumb through the thin lace. I hear it tear as she moans my name into the hot air. I shove the ripped panties into my pocket and look to my right and left before pulling out my dick.

"This has to be quick," I tell her and then kiss her neck ravenously. As though I'm starved for her. Her slender fingers grip into my shoulders as I wrap her legs around me and tease the head of my dick against her heat. I'm easing it in, sliding back and forth and she's already soaking wet.

The deep, gruff sound at the back of my throat is all for her as I push myself all the way in to the hilt in one swift stroke.

She cries out, slamming her head back, but it's muffled as she bites down into her lip.

I thrust upward as hard as I can, burying myself in her tight cunt. Fuck, she feels so damn good. She claws at my back as I slam into her, her back pushing against the wall each time.

My pace is steady, relentless and each pump of my hips has her climbing higher and higher.

Before I even feel the need to cum, she's already clamping down on my dick and whimpering her release.

It's the sweetest fucking sound I've ever heard. I want to hear it every damn day. I want her to cling to me like she needs me.

And to trust that I'll give it to her. I'll give her everything.

I pick up my pace, racing for my own release and riding through hers.

"So fucking good," I moan into the curve of her neck.

Nipping and kissing as I take her like I want her.

I meant for it to be quick, but I hold back just enough so I can make it last a little longer. I want to hold on to her. She needs to know that.

She's limp when I'm done with her. Her legs are trembling and I have to lean her against the wall so I can pull my pants back up. Her eyes are closed when I look up at her, and I don't think I've ever seen someone look so damn beautiful.

She doesn't fight me when I grip her chin between my thumb and forefinger, getting her attention so I can look her in the eyes and tell her, "Stop pushing me away. I don't like it."

Her chest is still heaving, but her shallow breath is starting to come back to her.

I wait a second for her to search my gaze, and I hope she finds what she's looking for because I mean it.

"I can give you everything you want, Allie. All you have to do is let me."

Chapter 17

Allison

"You know I'm no good, right?" I can't help but ask him as we sit next to each other in the diner. In the back of my head, I can hear myself saying he's no good for me too. But it's so quiet. The hum of something else has taken over. He gives me a fuzzy feeling. One I haven't felt in a long time. *One that makes me want more than what I'd planned.*

The food's half-gone on my plate. Just chicken tenders and fries. You can't go wrong with that. Dean's finished his burger and is working through the pile of fries left on his plate. A pair of Cokes top off the meal.

He huffs like it's a joke and doesn't answer me, reaching for his drink instead. I find it fascinating watching him. He's different. A kind of different I like.

He makes me feel safe and wanted. It's foolish, but I want that. *I want him.* All of him. And that's something I've never wanted before.

"I think this weekend I'm going away. I don't have to worry about you running off, do I?" he asks me.

"You probably should," I say as a joke. Judging by the expression on his face, he doesn't like my answer. "Where are you going?" I ask to change the subject. I like his smile the best. My skin pricks at the realization. Knowing that my own happiness is somehow attached to someone else's. I don't care for it because people come and go. They leave you, disappoint you. They die.

And then you're left all alone.

"To Brunswick. I think," he says.

"You think?" I ask him playfully, but my heart hurts. My mother's in Brunswick. All of it happened in Brunswick. I hate Brunswick.

"I haven't decided if I'm going yet."

I let out a small chuckle; it's more a breath of a laugh. "I swear I won't run off, so you can go," I tell him.

"I just wanted to hear you say it. Right now, you're mine. We don't need labels, but I'll be damned if I'll let you think I'm fine with you fucking someone else." His words are hard and brutish. Almost like a slap in my face.

"What if I want to?" I ask him, and he looks me square in

the eyes.

"Do you?"

No, I don't. I hesitate, and my heart seems to struggle with each second. I can't do this to him.

"I guess not. You fuck well enough," I say and stuff a fry into my mouth, hating how much it hurts me to play it off.

"I'm serious, Allie," he says and his voice is hard, with no room for negotiation. "I don't want to think about you just up and leaving."

"I don't even know you," I answer in jest, but all humor leaves me when I see the look in his eyes. They're dark, piercing. *Possessive.*

"Yeah, you do. You know enough." He lets out a heavy breath, pushing his plate away. "I'm telling you I want you and I don't want you running around on me. That's all I'm asking."

"I think I like that," I say, mesmerized by how easily he admitted that. How easily he made himself vulnerable. I really like it. "I want that too."

"You want me?" he asks with the hint of a smile and I nod, then say, "Yeah, I want you."

"Only me?" he asks, cocking a brow.

"Sure, for now," I answer him with a flirtation I think he likes.

The smile on my face only grows, as does his. That's the thing about him that's addictive. The pain vanishes when he smiles.

It's quiet for a minute. A long minute and I don't like the

tension, but I'm the one who caused it to begin with. A dull ache pulses between my legs as I lean closer to him and cross them.

"You did a number on me," I whisper and brush my cheek against his arm. My fingers play around his large wrist for a moment, just to feel him.

He's so close, only inches away since we're sitting on the same side of the booth. I guess he wanted to make sure I wasn't going to take off again. Smart of him.

"Is that right?" he says, putting down his drink so he can rest his hand on my thigh. We both watch as he rubs it with his thumb in slow, soothing circles. "How's your shoulder?" he asks me, and it takes a second to register.

Reaching up with my hand to push the fabric aside, I take a look and let out a small laugh. "I match you now," I tell him.

He brushes my hand away and gently soothes the scrape. I can hardly feel it; I barely feel anything but exhaustion at the moment.

"It's nothing," I tell him and he glances at me, but then back at my shoulder.

"Beds are better," he says with a small smile, but it doesn't reach his eyes. "Did you like it?" he asks me.

"Dean, you have no idea what I'd let you do to me." I shake my head and feel embarrassed by how quickly and honestly I responded. I should know better.

"Is that why you think you're no good? Because you like it hard?"

"Not just hard."

"Brutal, anal, gangbang, rape fantasy, what?" He says the words like they're no big deal. Maybe to him, they aren't. Some people, though ... some people use them to hurt others. "How fucking bad do you go, Allie Cat?" he asks me and I hesitate. So much is threatening to spill out. My heart's racing and my hands are feeling clammy.

"It's not as easy as me just picking a fantasy and you deliver," I tell him, watching my hands as I pick at my fingernails.

"Sure it is. Unless it's a gangbang situation you're after. It's going to be hard for me to fill that order by my lonesome."

I snicker and slowly shake my head, finally peeking up at him.

"I like to fuck," he says as he leans in closer to me. "And I'll tell you a little secret," he whispers as he lowers his lips to my ear. "I've done dirtier shit and loved it."

"Like what?" I ask him instantly, desperate to know.

"I've used rope before," he finally answers before reaching for his soda and taking a drink. My eyes lift to his, willing him to continue. "I like having control. So long as I have that, I can push the boundaries. I can chase you down, pin you beneath me. You need to tell me what you want, but if you think you're oh so bad, little kitten, I can assure you that you're not."

He has no idea that he's the one playing with fire, not me.

"I just like ..." I pause but force myself to look him in the eyes as I continue, "to fight back." It's a secret I haven't told anyone else. I want to play. I want to push my limits. I haven't met someone I could do it with. Not until Dean.

"You didn't fight me much out there," he responds, and a spark of desire ignites within me.

"Did you want me to?" I ask him and he shrugs in response, picking at the fries on his plate.

"I don't care how I fuck you so long as I get to," he answers me with a slowly growing smirk on his face.

I find it hard to focus. To eat. To do anything other than think about how much Dean could push me, and how I could push him right back.

Chapter 18

Dean

She's a little kitten, my Allie Cat. She thinks she's so dirty and bad, but really she just likes rough and hard sex. It's cute. Well, as long as she listens it's cute. As long as she stays where she belongs.

The first step after dinner was to take a look at the kind of porn she's into. She can get all quiet and shy talking about it, but her search history doesn't hide a damn thing.

Brutal fuck.

Hard rough fuck.

Choked, slapped, punished.

I huff a small laugh when I see her phone on the nightstand. She brought up a picture of a girl all tied up with rope.

Fuck that. My answer: *I don't have time for that shit.* She got a kick out of my reaction. Maybe I'll tie her ass up for Christmas or something if we're still together then, but right now, I just need her ass to sit pretty.

Yeah, she's a little kitten. And she deserves to be fucked however she wants it. Just thinking about it is getting my dick hard again. Even with the knowledge she's passed out and her cunt's sore and swollen from the hard fuck I just gave her.

Her sweet smell drifts toward me as she cuddles in close. She's only got a twin bed and her bedroom looks like she just moved in. There's just a bed and a dresser full of clothes.

It reminds me of my room after my father died and we moved.

I clear my throat and wrap my arm around her small form, pressing her soft body into mine. Her little murmur of satisfaction stops the thoughts of my father in their tracks.

Thank fuck for that, but I still can't sleep.

It's almost 3:00 a.m. and I'm wide awake, although I don't know why. I should've exhausted myself into a coma, but I can't turn off thinking about everything that's happened this week. It's been fast and furious with Allie. I'm not the type that gets attached. This girl is getting to me, and I don't know why. I can't explain it.

A low groan rumbles in the back of my throat as I remember how I made her get down on all fours with her ass in the air, all so I could watch my cum leak out of her pretty little pussy.

Another groan, another memory. My dick twitches and hardens with need. The last straw is when she throws her leg over my thigh and her bare pussy rubs against me.

"You doing that on purpose?" I ask her and the little minx smiles. Guess I'm not the only one who can't sleep.

I push her onto her back and nuzzle her neck to wake her up.

"I want you," I tell her and nip her ear. Her palms push weakly against my chest until I rock my hard dick against her pussy. My lips drop to the crook of her neck as I moan, "You're so fucking wet."

She mewls an incoherent response.

Getting on my knees, I try to push her onto her stomach, but she protests. "What if I want you like this?" she asks me. Her eyes are half-lidded, and her hair's a messy halo scattered across the pillow.

She digs her heels into my ass as she spreads her thighs for me. "Just like this."

My heart beats harder. "Just on top?" I tease her, letting my fingers trail up her thigh to the dip in her waist. The shiver that runs through her body makes me smile.

She gives me a simple nod and props herself up on her elbows so I can wrap my arms around her back. Nestling my hips against hers, I line up my dick and slide in gently.

"Nice and slow," she says softly, sleep evident in her voice. Her head falls back the second I push inside of her.

I'm gentle at first, letting the bed rock with us in slow motions. It hits the wall every time. I thought we'd managed to put a hole in the drywall with the last round.

The smell of sex fills the air as I keep up a steady pace. I'm deliberately holding back. Forcing her to writhe under me and dig her heels into my ass harder.

She cries out a strangled plea for more. I can feel her cunt tighten, but she'll never get off like this. Not for a while at least.

She's breathless when she looks up at me. "Harder," she begs me.

And I give her just what she wants, feeling her heart race against mine.

I lift her up on her side first, straddling her leg so I can push all the way into her without her hips hitting mine. The second I slide into her, still gentle with my thrust, her plump lips part with a gasp and she grips the comforter as she screams out.

"Dean!" she cries out my name as I slam into her again. A deep, rough noise is forced from me when I feel the head of my dick bump against her cervix.

Fuck yes.

I pound into her again and again, gripping onto her thigh with a bruising force to keep her right where I want her. Even as she tries to move away from me.

She pushes against me, struggling and writhing with the intensity of what I'm what doing to her. It's almost too much. Her nails scratch at my chest and dig into my skin. Her face scrunches with a mixture of pain and pleasure, but I don't hold back. Bending down, I kiss her jaw and she's eager to meet my lips with hers. It's hot and heavy and different. Different between us and electric.

I can feel she's close from the way her pussy tightens and from the sweet sounds she's making. I fucking love it. I love what I can do to her.

"Dean, fuck!" she yells out as her neck arches and her head digs into the pillow. I lean closer to her so I can bite down on her neck, sucking and nipping as I push her higher and higher. A small whimper is followed by a sibilant sound on her lips. I can hear the word *stop* on the tip of her tongue. It's the smallest hint of this being too much for her, making me pull back slightly. Only slightly, and I keep up my pace.

My heart beats hard and fast, desperate for more but knowing she's on the edge of it hurting her, of being too much. It's for her. I can hardly breathe as I wait in that short moment where I know I've pushed too hard.

She doesn't miss a beat though, completely oblivious to the fact that I'm taking it easy on her. She's a tight fit and feels too damn good to stop.

The bed slams into the wall and her fingers cling to my shoulders, urging me on but still fighting me.

She pushes against me and writhes with the need to get away; it's so fucking intense, but I don't stop. I need more.

More of this. *More of her.*

"Dean!" she screams out my name as her cunt spasms on my cock and her body goes rigid, paralyzed from pleasure.

"Thank fuck," I whisper against her neck, feeling her heat surround me as I hammer into her over and over, ruthlessly fucking her deeper and deeper as her arousal leaks between us.

I ride through her orgasm and take what's mine until I feel the telltale signs of my own release.

Her blunt nails scratch into my shoulder as I thrust deeply one last time and feel thick hot streams leave me in waves.

"Allie." It's all I can manage to say as my body rocks with the thrill of my release.

When I finally come back down, Allie's legs are shaking and she's still trembling beneath me with her own pleasure.

My mouth is dry and my heart racing as I slip out of her, letting our combined cum drip down her thigh.

"Oh my God," Allie murmurs as she turns on her side and curls up.

All I feel is pride as I pull the covers over her. She's still shaking.

"You all right?" I question and she nods her head, but keeps her eyes tightly shut. "You're on the pill, right?" I ask her as I stand up and grab my shirt to wipe myself off and then go back to clean her up.

I finally feel spent, but I should've asked about the pill days ago.

She shakes her head, and I stand there dumbfounded for a moment.

It's quiet. Allie's still in the same position.

"You need me to go get you some Plan B or something?" I say and try to figure out how many days or hours that shit works for.

She laughs into her pillow and then winces as she rolls onto her back and pulls the covers up tighter around her. "On the shot, dummy," she says and it's only then I let out a breath.

"Well shit, you could have led with that."

The sweet cadence of her joyful laugh fills the night air.

"You think you're funny," I tell her and she's quick to respond with, "You're the one who jokes so much."

"Yeah well, sad people like to rely on humor," I say without thinking. A chill flows over my skin, hating that I just said that. I don't know what Allie does to me, but goddamn does she bring out a side of me no one else gets to see.

"That's funny, because I never joke," she says without missing a beat, parting her legs for me when I slip the shirt between her thighs.

"You sad, Allie Cat?" I ask, wiping her up and then tossing the shirt into the hamper in the bathroom. She doesn't answer me. Maybe she says shit to me she shouldn't too. That'd only be fair.

"You know I'm going to break down your walls," I whisper against her lips and then slide beneath the covers with her on this tiny bed. I can feel the weight of exhaustion already pulling me under.

"I wish you wouldn't," she says but presses her body against mine, nuzzling next to me and wrapping her arm around my abs.

"Maybe that's why I want to so bad."

Chapter 19

Allison

I feel so deliciously used.

My nipples harden every time I feel that deep ache between my thighs, which is practically every time I move.

Even now, as I slide into my chair on the right side of the classroom. I'm early for once in my life. And I'm grateful the only other person here to see me and my sit of shame is Angie.

"Ooh," she says, making a perfect O with her mouth and then snickers as she slips the bookbag off her shoulders. "Looks like you're having a good time, huh?"

I haven't spoken to her since that first time, even though she's been friendly.

I just don't make friends. Or have them. I don't want them, and I wouldn't make a good friend in return either. So, there's no point.

But I've never been too good to brag.

"You could say that," I respond with an expression of pure content and a Cheshire cat smile.

"So ..." she says, "who is he?" She talks while opening her textbook followed by her notebook, filled with what looks like an actual outline and highlighted words.

It's obvious she actually gives a fuck about chemistry or at least about passing the class. Good for her.

Before I can even open my mouth, I catch a glimpse of Dean from the corner of my eye. With his height and broad shoulders, he takes up the whole doorframe before walking in. I can feel my body react to his. The way my heart skips, my thighs tighten. I'm more than acutely aware of his presence.

I bite down on my lip, raise a brow and nod my head in his direction although I keep my eyes on Angie's.

I can hear him stride across the room and take the seat next to mine, but all the while Angie's expression drops. Her back stiffens and she forces a smile that's not genuine.

"Just be careful," she mutters without looking me in the eye and then goes back to her notes.

That's not the reaction I was expecting, and my gaze lingers on her longer than it should.

I don't like it. Not in the least.

During the entire class, I can't help but to glance at her. I'm still trying to make sense of her reaction but she ignores me entirely.

Even when Dean puts his hand on my thigh. Even when he leans over and covertly whispers dirty little promises in my ear. My focus is on Angie, who looks more and more uncomfortable even though she's not looking at us.

Before we're even halfway through class I pass him a note and feel like I'm back in fucking high school. This ... whatever this is between us, is stupid. All of it. But I guess I'm the stupid one really because I keep falling for this shit with Dean.

The question is simple; did you fuck her?

I get a what-the-fuck expression in return from him, paired with a furious headshake and then a cocky smirk. The note he sends back pisses me off. He likes that I'm jealous.

I'm not fucking jealous.

This right here, this is why I don't have friends. Or boyfriends or fuck buddies or *anyone* in my life. I don't need the spiked lump in my throat that makes me wish I had more water in the bottle in my bag so I could take a large gulp. Or maybe vodka in the bottle. I could use a shot to get rid of this tension.

I have to force myself to relax and the moment I do, finally listening to the professor, Angie gives me a friendly smile. Genuine. Maybe I'm just crazy.

I'm irritated, all because of one look from a girl I don't even know. That's not me. Just as I'm shaking it off, Dean's heavy hand lands on my desk holding a scrap of paper meant only for my eyes.

You want a list of the girls I've fucked?

"Oh my God, shut up." I don't hide my irritation as I mumble the response.

Professor Grant glances our way as Dean chuckles. At least he's having a good time with it all.

He lowers his hand to my thigh again, scooting his desk closer to mine as quietly as he can. He's a big brute in that tiny desk and can't do a damn thing quietly. I don't know why it makes me smile like it does. He plays it off, mouthing he's sorry to the professor and I find myself trying to bite back the humor.

But I instantly realize why he moved closer when he slips his hand onto my thigh.

I should look to see if the professor sees, or maybe even Angie. My dirty mind looks to see what time it is and quickly calculates how many minutes are left before class will be over.

When I peek at him, knowing there are only ten minutes or so remaining, he's sinking his teeth into his lower lip, giving me a sexy grin as he squeezes my upper thigh and then lets his fingers drift closer and closer to where they want to be.

I'm in jeans so there's no way he's going to be doing anything too scandalous. I like his ownership of me. I like that he likes me and doesn't mind showing people.

I like that I like him too.

Even if Angie has a stick up her ass about it. Or not ... what do I know?

And so I part my thighs just a bit, enough for him to slip his fingertips all the way up, pressing the seam of the jeans against my clit.

My breath hitches and I look straight ahead as if my body isn't igniting under his touch.

He doesn't try to get me off, and he's gentle more than anything else. Petting me and pausing when my eyes close.

It's over before it really gets started, though.

The sound of everyone packing up is the cue he needs to pull back his hand. I'm riding a high from the forbidden foreplay and I don't acknowledge her when Angie says goodbye. I hear her, but I pretend I don't. Maybe that makes me callous or catty or something else. It doesn't matter. I didn't come here to make friends.

Although I didn't come here for Dean either.

We're the last two remaining. It's becoming a habit. One I'm starting to grow fond of.

"What's going on tonight?" he asks me, and I don't answer.

He's a tornado. Destructive and all-consuming. And just like a natural disaster, I'm not quite sure how to handle Dean or if I can use this situation to my advantage.

One thing is certain, there's going to be a path of wreckage left in his wake.

"I'm staying home this weekend I think," I answer him honestly. I'll be alone in the house, planning and considering all my options.

"Like at your parents' place?" he asks me.

"No, just here." The thought of going home to my

mother's is one I don't give the time of day.

"Got it," he says, moving his bookbag he didn't even touch to the top of his desk.

"Well, I'm heading out early tomorrow morning. You want to hang out tonight?" he asks me and then winks. *He's not going to be here this weekend.* My heart slams hard against my rib cage, although on the surface I keep my body relaxed. I had plans. Plans that were easy because he'd be at the frat party. But maybe this means I can save him from all this. Maybe it's meant to be this way.

"Come on, don't make me go to bed all alone," Dean says and pouts when I don't answer fast enough for him.

I can't help but laugh.

"You want to fuck me but not bring me home to your mother, that it?" I tease him back.

"You want to come? I'll bring you."

"You're fucking crazy." My laugh is joined by the zip of my bag as I close it.

"I'm not staying there long; you want to come with?"

"I don't think I'm the type of girl you bring home to your parents." *And I have things planned.* I don't tell him that part. He can't know.

"First, you're blind and delusional. Second, I hate my mother."

"So, bringing me home would be to spite her?" Suddenly feeling lightened by the situation, a smirk graces my face. "Like to piss her off?" It's another game.

"You're something else, you know that?" he says, not answering my question.

If only he knew.

"What about rugby? Don't you guys have a game or something?" I ask him, feeling a stir of anxiety deep in my stomach. It radiates outward as he answers.

"It's not important, and the guys know I'm leaving. I'm not an official member anyway. It was just Kevin's idea that I join."

"You close to Kevin?" I ask him.

"His uncle really. He's paying my ride here."

"Why?" Shifting my backpack to rebalance the weight of the heavy books, I wait for an answer. I didn't know that. It's not something I would have been able to look up online, but damn I don't like it.

"I got into some stuff, beat a guy pretty fucking bad and Jack's friends with both my uncle and the judge. He said he'd watch me and offered to 'set me straight.'" He huffs a laugh but it's obvious that Dean's grateful for it.

"He sounds like a good guy." I breathe out the words although I feel empty saying them.

"It's a favor to my uncle. Not that I don't appreciate it."

He runs his fingers along his stubble as he looks up at the clock. He's got another class to attend and we're already taking too long in this empty room, but I have to ask. "Why'd you get into a fight with that other guy?"

"He was just getting a little too handsy."

"With you?" I joke, but he doesn't even smile.

There's a hardness about Dean, just beneath his cocky and facetious exterior. "With this chick. I was drunk and so were they. Turns out she was his wife."

"He was just flirting with his wife and you beat the shit out of him?" I say but again he doesn't laugh.

"If flirting means grabbing her by the hair to pull her out of the bar, then yeah. Sure."

"Why the hell did you get locked up then?" I ask him, feeling my heart drop at the image of what he's describing playing in my head.

"She lied. She didn't want her husband to go to jail."

Sickness coils in my stomach. "I'm sorry."

"Yo," I hear someone call out and turn to see Daniel in the doorway.

He nods at Dean, his face cleanly shaven and his hair pushed back. "You got a minute?" he asks Dean and my heart hammers hard and fast, like I've just been caught in a lie.

Daniel doesn't even look at me. It makes me wonder if he knows something he shouldn't. Or if I'm maybe missing a piece to the puzzle.

"One sec," Dean says quietly and then plants a kiss on my jaw before leaving me behind. It's odd what one little kiss will do.

Knowing before he left, he had to leave me with one little kiss.

I just hope it's not my last.

Chapter 20

Dean

Pissed off is something I'm used to.

Enraged, irate, resentful.

But none of them compare to how I feel right now.

"You can't even really tell it's her," Daniel says and I don't trust myself to answer just yet. I can't even take my eyes away from the picture on the phone.

"You think she'll be upset?" he asks me.

Do I think Allison is going to be upset that a picture of her riding my dick by the dumpsters at the diner is on the university's social media accounts and it's circulating like wildfire? Yes. Yes, I fucking do. You can't identify me in the picture, but her? Clear as day. At least to me.

I grit my teeth and flex my jaw, looking over my shoulder and back at Allie.

"Yeah," I answer him with one word as my heated blood pumps harder. "I fucked up," I tell him, wiping a hand down my face. The anger is nothing compared to the feeling of knowing something I did is going to hurt her.

I fucking loved what I did to her in that moment.

And I know she loved it too.

"Don't read the comments. It's just going to set you off." I glance up at him before scrolling and reading through the messages. "I know how you are," Daniel adds. "Just ignore them," he tells me and reaches for the phone, but I push him back. Just one shove, just enough to tell him to back off.

What a slut.

She's getting fucked by the dumpsters like the trash she is.

That bitch is dirty.

I wonder if there's a line for that whore out there now.

Every comment makes my anger feel closer to spiraling out of control.

"Seriously, people talk shit. It's what they do. It's not like they can even tell it's her." Daniel keeps rambling, trying to calm me down but all I can see is red.

"They're not going to know it's her. She's fine."

"I don't want to show her this," I admit to Daniel, my throat tight and my muscles even tighter.

"I mean ... you might want to give her a heads-up. Just in

case?" he suggests and I know he's right, but fuck that.

"A heads-up about what?" Allison's voice is happy but reserved as she walks up to the two of us right outside the classroom door.

My back stiffens.

She shifts the strap of her backpack as a few people walk past us, heading out of their classes and toward the stairs. "Everything okay?" she asks, looking up at me.

Fuck. "You know you're late now, right?" she questions but the wary look on her beautiful face tells me she knows being late doesn't mean shit right now.

When I don't answer, Daniel chimes in. "What's going on?" he asks her.

She shrugs. "Not much. What's going on with you?"

"Same," he says and then it's awkward. "Not much." Real fucking awkward as she looks between the two of us.

"Some shit happened," I tell her, forcing out the words. I try to keep my words even, although my chest feels tight and I don't know if I'm breathing. I only just got her ass to settle down. And now this?

"I'm sorry," I tell her and Allie's smooth forehead pinches with a deep crease. Again she shifts the strap, holding on to it with both her hands.

"What is it?" she asks me in a hollow voice.

Daniel and I exchange a look before I hand Allie his phone.

It takes her a moment to register what she's looking at, a

long moment but then her eyes go wide, and she covers her mouth with her hand.

"Oh my God!" she breathes through her hand and then uncovers it to reveal a bit of a smile. "I look so fat," she says comically as if it's a holiday portrait of her.

"You can always go back and I'll take a different one," Daniel jokes and I want to smack the fucker upside his head.

"These people are assholes," Allie says as she scrolls through the comments like it's no big deal.

I'm surprised she isn't shaken in the least. Not pissed off at all like I am. She's a strong girl, I know that, but still. The comments are brutal. She hasn't even read them all. Her smile dims but she isn't pissed, she isn't angry, she isn't hurt. If she is, she's good at hiding it.

Daniel's smiling like a fool. "Well if it makes you feel any better, the picture doesn't make me think about you any differently than I did before." His comment makes Allie laugh but not me.

"Fuck off," I tell him.

Daniel puts both hands up. "Just trying to lighten the mood," he says although his eyes darken slightly. He's good at joking, but it's only a facade. I know one when I see one.

"It's fine," Allie says easily, handing Daniel his phone back. "Seriously, I don't care. You can't even tell it's me, can you?"

"Nope. That's what I told the Hulk over here," Daniel says, and I glare at him.

"The Hulk?" Allie smiles. "Is that what they call you?" she asks me.

"It's a stupid fucking nickname."

"It's because he gets pissed so often," Daniel says to Allie, sliding his phone into his back pocket and then looking up at me, but someone else catches his eye.

"Anyway, I'm going to head out," he says to both of us although he's watching some chick. I get a quick look at her walking down the stairs and when I look back at him, his gaze is fixated on her. I don't think I've seen her before.

"Hey, thanks," I tell him before he heads off chasing whomever she is.

"Yeah, no problem," he says and then finally looks back at me. "Seriously, it's not a big deal. Just thought you'd want a heads-up."

"Thanks, Daniel," Allie calls after him as he stalks away in the opposite direction of that chick. "Delete that from your spank bank, please." I love her smile and humor, but not right now. Not when I know a piece of her has to be hurting.

If only she'd admit it.

"You sure you're all right?" I ask her.

"Yeah, I don't care."

I lean against the wall as I consider her. "Not even a little?"

"Nope," she says, really emphasizing the word and her mouth lets out a little *pop* as she does. "It is a little dirty and it's not like voyeurism isn't trending right now ... but I know who I am and they don't. They just want to feel better about themselves. That's the only reason for saying those things. I'll admit I'm happy you can't really see my face," she says, lowering her voice as she walks closer to me, letting her hands settle against my chest. "And you kind of look hot from that view. It's not one I get to see."

I let out a hint of a chuckle and give her the response she wants.

"If you want, I'll track down the asshole who shared it," I offer her. I don't add that I'll be breaking his fucking phone over his little prick head.

"Seriously, Dean. It's not that big of a deal."

She leans against the brick wall, her bookbag squished behind her. "It's nothing I haven't heard before. Pretty sure most women hear it at some point." Letting out a short laugh, she adds, "Maybe not for fucking where people can see …" She gets up on her tiptoes and plants a small kiss on my lips as if to end the conversation.

I don't like it.

I don't like it at all.

"Your ass is coming with me this weekend," I tell her, and her mouth opens in surprise. It's the possessiveness in me that made up my mind. If I'm going, she's going.

"I'm coming with you?" She repeats my statement like it's a question although her brow raises like it's a challenge.

"Yes," I say sternly, wrapping my hand around her waist

and crushing her into my chest. "I want you to come with me." My skin tingles with the heat of anxiety.

I anticipate a fight, but I get a sweet, "Okay," and a quick peck on the lips.

I guess I'm really going now.

Chapter 21

Allison

There's an uneasiness in the pit of my stomach.

That's what makes me so aware that everything is wrong and off-kilter.

I know it when I get into Dean's car. I'm conscious of it in every fiber of my body as I click the seat belt into place. This unsettled feeling won't leave. I know something bad is going to happen.

But he keeps smiling at me.

So, I swallow it down and try to breathe.

It's partly because I'm so fucking aware that I want more of him. That I'm on the verge of giving him whatever he'd want, just to keep him. That's the crux of it. I want him. And more than that, I want him to want me.

The car engine clicks over and the radio booms to life. I keep telling myself that I can pretend. I lie and tell myself I'll like pretending.

I think I've lied so much up to this point that I'm not even sure what's real anymore.

"This song blows," I say, reaching for the stereo just to fuck with him and distract myself, but Dean smacks my hand away. It stings for a moment and I feign a pained expression.

"My car, my radio," he says, completely deadpan.

"Seriously," I tell him, giving up on switching the dial since he keeps thwacking me with the back of his hand. "I'm not listening to this for two hours." My brow is raised and the most serious of expressions is on my face.

"You have to be kidding." Dean stares at me with a look of despair in his eyes and I finally break my composure, settling back into the seat and kicking off my flip-flops so I can sit cross-legged.

"Yeah, I am. This is the only station I actually like up here." I can't hold back my smile as that familiar warm feeling flows through me. The one where I give a damn about how my words will be taken. If he gets me.

I've heard Dean laugh a few times and usually it's this sexy, deep and rough chuckle that seems to vibrate up his chest, but this laugh, this is different. It's easy as he throws his head back and gives me a handsome smile.

It's a dangerous look because it makes me smile too.

"Thank fuck," he says and then he turns the radio down before putting the car into reverse. It's at that volume level where you know the other person wants to talk. Right now, I don't like that level. I'd rather blare music the whole way down.

"Hey, I like that song," I tease him but he ignores me. The car moves easily out of the spot in the parking garage and for the first time since this trip came up, I start questioning it.

Dean clears his throat and puts the car into drive.

"You all right?" I ask him, feeling a sense of wariness grow in my chest.

"My mom's kind of a bitch," he tells me and as much as that sucks, I'm happy to hear that's what's making his face look all uncomfortable.

"I think that's normal maybe?" I say and take another look around the car. The bags are in the back seat, but he doesn't want to stay long and assured me we're *absolutely not* staying at his mother's. Which is nice, because fuck staying over at someone's mother's house. That's a given.

Next to my duffle bag, there's a white plastic shopping bag.

"What's in the bag?" I ask Dean.

He glances at me and then blows out a short huff of a laugh. "I picked up a shirt. For you." He examines my expression, watching to see how I react.

"From where?" I ask him as I reach into the back seat, taking the bag and reading the drugstore label on the bag.

"From the mall, it's just in that bag because it was laying around."

The wide and joyful smile on my face won't budge. I lift the fabric out of the bag. It's simple white cotton, but high quality. It's not quite like the one he ruined, but it's pretty and soft. I'm sure I could make it look dirty, though.

Even as my playful banter and perverted thoughts try to shove it all down, this little feeling pricks up, making me hot and uncomfortable. A feeling I want to reject. Immediately. Or at least I would have before.

"I didn't know your size but—" he says and I cut him off before he can continue.

"I love it." I wait for his gaze to meet mine before I lean across the small car and plant a chaste kiss on his lips. "You didn't have to, you know?" I say, slipping the shirt back into the bag and setting it down in the back seat again.

"Well, I'm happy it made you smile."

The comfortable silence between us comes and then goes. Whatever's eating him makes the air tense in this small car. "So, your mom?" I prod him for more information.

"She's just," he says then pauses and the sound of the turn signal, the steady clicking, fills the cabin. We slow to a stop at a crosswalk and he looks at me. "We haven't gotten along in a long time, but my," he says as his eyes flicker to mine and then back to the road before the car moves again and he continues, "my anger management therapist ..." he trails off after saying the words slowly.

"Your shrink?" I say and when he quirks a brow and gauges my expression I give him a comforting smile. "What's your shrink say about her?"

"Not much. He thinks I should go see her, though."

I pick at my nails and peek up at Dean. Freshly shaven. I hadn't noticed that before. "Has it been a while since you've seen her?" I ask him and suddenly feel way too uncomfortable.

We're not even ten miles from his place. We have hours to drive. This conversation is a little too heavy for comfort.

But ... I'm curious. I can't deny that. What the hell did she do to him?

"Yeah, it's been a while," he says and his answer's short. Maybe it's heavy for him too, but that only makes me want to push him more.

"How long's a while?" I ask him.

"I left home when I was sixteen."

"Sixteen is a good age for change," I mumble, looking out of the window as he turns onto the highway and finally picks up speed. The trees blur by and I keep talking before Dean can comment. "When was the last time you saw her?"

He doesn't look at me as he switches lanes and answers, "When I was sixteen."

"Damn."

"Yeah," he says and then adds, "I probably should've told you."

"I mean ... I'd have thought it would have come up in

conversation, maybe?" I say jokingly but really, what the fuck?

"I wasn't going to go, but then I wanted to get away after that picture. And I wanted to take you with me."

"So you just figured it'd be fine to drop it all on me once I was securely fastened in your car?"

He shrugs, making the shirt that's already tight across his shoulders look that much tighter. "It seemed like a sign, I guess." His words come out soft and they're nearly drowned out by the faint music and the sound of the air conditioner, but I heard them.

"Anyway, I just wanted to apologize since it may be a little weird. But you asked for this," he adds, lightening his tone and trying to be playful.

My heart thuds and feels like it's flipping. Like it's trying to move inside my chest. It takes a moment for me to realize it's because I'm not breathing. "Yeah, I did."

"So, it's normal for moms to be bitches?" Dean asks me, and I glance at him in my periphery, picking at my nails. That's all he's getting right now. He doesn't let up though, eager to push the conversation. "I'm guessing mine's going to be worse than yours."

"I was just trying to make you feel better," I respond half-heartedly, and he gets a chuckle out of it that makes me smile.

"Well, shit," he answers and then glances up at the large green sign on the side of the road.

"So?" I say, drawing out the word.

"What?"

"What'd she do that made her a bitch?"

"Oh," he says and his tone drops again. "She just is." I nod once, thinking he's going to leave it there. But as I pull a book out of my bag to read, committed to sitting in silence the entire trip, Dean proves me wrong.

"I didn't think she was when I was younger."

"Most kids love their moms." I think about how my mom was my hero. She was the one who was supposed to make it all better.

"She was bad with money; my parents were always fighting about it." He glances at me and then asks, "You really want to know?"

Placing my hand on the book in my lap, I tell him, "Consider me the in-car shrink. Tell me everything."

"There's not much to tell. My mom's a greedy bitch. My dad got sick and my mom cashed in on his insurance."

"Is he okay?" I ask hesitantly, and Dean shakes his head.

"He died a long time ago," he tells me and before I can even tell him I'm sorry, before I can share that my dad's gone too, he keeps talking. I recognize the nature of his voice, how it's like a story. Someone else's story he's telling. It's so he can pretend it doesn't affect him anymore. And that makes the wound that much deeper. "She couldn't wait for it to come. She married a guy more well-off than my father," he says and then lowers his voice to continue, "who was a fucking asshole."

I'd laugh at his tone and the way he said it, but he can't hide the pain in his eyes.

He keeps going. "And then he died, so now she's all alone."

"Your stepdad?"

"Yeah, his name was Rick."

"She has bad luck with men," I tell him in a monotone and then quickly add, "I'm sorry. "

"It's all right. Rick was an asshole and a drunk."

"Well, about your dad and everything. I'm really sorry." I mean every word and that unsettled feeling that bothered me when we first got in this car comes back, but I push it down.

It's not about me right now. That thought makes it feel better.

He tries to shrug it off but I feel compelled to at least reach out to him. Shifting in my seat so I'm leaning close enough to him, I rest my hand on his thigh. My fingers move rhythmically against the rough denim. "I really am sorry."

A warmth spreads through every inch of me when Dean covers my hand with his, his other twisting on the steering wheel. His touch on my hand starts at the very tips of my fingers but then spreads when he picks up my hand and kisses the tips of my fingers ever so gently. His gaze never strays from the road. He's a beast of a man. A brute. It makes the soft touches that much more meaningful.

He sets my hand back down and it's soothing. Deep inside of me, something feels not so broken anymore. Like a kindled fire come back to life.

"I'm all right," he says like that's the end of it. But I want more now.

There's something about knowing other people's shit that comforts me. Like if they can go through all that and come out okay, then maybe I'll be all right. It's why I like to read thrillers and dark romances. No matter how bad it gets, when it ends, usually there's a happily ever after. That doesn't happen every time, though.

"Why does your anger management therapist," I say, repeating the words like he said them but it doesn't budge the stern expression on his face, "want you to go see her?"

"My uncle called and said I should see go her since Rick died. He said she's not handling it well."

"So, not awkward at all," I say then shrug and try to bring back the playfulness.

His rough chuckle eases the tension that's nearly suffocating me; the feeling that we're rapidly approaching being too close. "I told her I'd just stop by but that we also had other plans."

"What plans?" I ask him.

"Maybe we go to dinner and you tell me your story?" he suggests, taking a quick peek at me.

Shaking my head and ignoring my racing heart, I answer quickly, "So, you want to be bored to death?"

"I know there's something there," he says and I feel like a monster. Guilt and regret creep up my body in a slow wave.

"Nothing that's interesting."

"You don't always have to brush things off. It's okay to let someone in, you know?" As he talks, he periodically looks at me. Like he's gauging my reaction.

"I think I'm good."

"It took a lot for me to tell you about my mom. You could open up a little too."

"I did that once. Like I said, I think I'm good," I tell him as I pull my knees to my chest, stretching the seat belt over them and looking out of the window.

"I'm guessing it didn't end well?" he says.

"Nope." My answer is simple, my voice high pitched and peppy, but inside I'm screaming. Inside it hurts. All the pain is wound up and coiled into barbed wire, cutting me open and wishing I would spill it all. I told my mom. And it was supposed to get better. She was supposed to make it all better.

"Well, who was it you told?" He's keeping his voice light and acting like he's just making small talk, but I can see right through him.

"No one you know," I tell him and feel guilty for not confiding in him. I usually don't care if I disappoint someone, but Dean is different.

"You know how I just said it's okay to let people in?" he reminds me with a smirk and then rests his hand on my thigh when I don't respond. He rubs his fingers back and forth in soothing strokes. Like he's comforting me. It feels like a setup.

Silence greets me, backs me into a corner. Waiting for me to make the next move.

"It's not fair that you decided to make this trip a fucking therapy session."

His laugh is brief before he replies, "Life's a therapy session, Allie Cat." He doesn't move his hand, he just keeps it on my thigh and I find myself wanting to put my hand on top of his and run my thumb along his knuckles.

"Sam ... Sam is who I let in." I give him that small bit of information even though it's not quite what he asked. He asked who I told. I gave him who I let in. Big difference, but he doesn't need to know that. Hearing her name makes me feel like I've betrayed her. Has it been that long since I've said her name out loud?

"What'd he do?" Dean asks and I let out a genuine laugh, pretending the tears in the corners of my eyes are from humor.

"Sam as in Samantha."

"Oh, a chick?" Dean leans forward and then relaxes back in his seat, clearly not expecting that. "So, was this like, a thing?" he asks me, and the smile stays plastered on my lips.

"Sorry to disappoint you, but I'm only into dick."

"Got it," Dean says. "She was a friend?"

I just nod and look back out the window although I don't really see anything. Blurs of scenary as we make our way along the highway. I remember when Sam and I met in preschool. We were so young and stupid, fighting over some rainbow eraser until the teacher took it away and made us share a plain one. Back when everything was okay, and we were just kids. When "best friends for life" meant something special.

"What was she like?" he asks me. Dean isn't getting the hint but for some reason, I like it. Maybe it's the memories or the soothing sound of the engine rumbling and the wind passing by the car. Or maybe it's just been a while since I've thought of Sam back before the night that changed everything happened.

It takes me a moment to think of the best way to answer him. "A lot like me," I start, although it's not quite right. I'm just pretending to be a lot like her.

"Big boobs. She was gifted with them." I add that difference humorously and I think about stopping there, but I don't. "She had the most beautiful smile and laugh. She used to joke that she was going to be a dentist because everyone would pay big bucks for a smile like hers. And she laughed at everything and it was real." I remember how happy she always was. "She was just a very confident, happy person."

"Sounds like a good friend," he says after a moment.

"Keep your eyes on the road," I scold him when I notice he's spending more time looking at me than he is paying attention to driving.

"What happened?" he asks me.

"My mom didn't want us hanging out," I tell him and I'm surprised how easily I said it. Like it doesn't feel like my heart is shattered by the memory. "We were just girls, fourteen and fifteen at the time."

"Why's that?"

"People said some things. Blamed some things that happened on Sam, and my mom said it was her fault." My voice cracks and I feel myself breaking down, so I reach for the volume on the stereo again. I turn it up, feeling guilty about so much and not wanting to deal with it.

Guilty about what happened back then.

Guilty about what's going to happen.

"Hey," Dean says softly, and I just barely hear him over the constant bass of whatever song this is. I don't recognize it. I glance at him, wishing I could hide, but he does that thing again, taking my hand and kissing the tips of my fingers. "You did good, Allie Cat."

If guilt could kill someone, I'd be dead.

Chapter 22

Dean

This is a bad idea.

The shrink was wrong. Driving all the way to 24 Easton Avenue in Brunswick wasn't anything I needed. As I watch my mother, who's sitting on the steps of the porch taking another puff of her cigarette, I already know I'm not going to get anything from her. And that this was a bad idea.

Closure, mending fences—whatever the hell Dr. Robinson thought I'd get from this isn't here.

My mother looks the same in a lot of ways but also beaten down, as if the years haven't been kind to her, or maybe I just remember her differently. She's in loose-fitting clothes that make her seem even smaller than when I saw her last. She looks frail beneath them.

Dr. Robinson is just like everyone else, thinking I'm exaggerating or that my perception is skewed. But showing up out of nowhere to tell my mother I'm working on my anger and making progress was a fucking mistake.

Allie stretches in her seat, slowly waking up from the nap she took for the last thirty minutes of the drive.

She's so damn beautiful when she sleeps.

I wish she'd stayed asleep, so I could keep driving.

"We're here?" she asks sleepily and tries to hide her yawn. I watch her look up at the house we're parked in front of. The seat protests as she leans forward and takes in the porch, a red and blue wreath adorning the front door and two matching pots with baby's breath on either side of it. "It's cute," she says sweetly.

I gesture across the street to my mother's place with my hand as it rests on the steering wheel and then turn off the ignition. "That one."

She's quick to turn her head and say it's cute too. And maybe it's all right on the outside. No homey details and it looks just like it did six years ago when my mother bought it with that asshole. Only more weathered... just like my mother.

"You can stay here if you want," I say. My anxiety is getting the best of me. I told Dr. Robinson I'd do it, so I will. I'm not a little bitch. But no one likes being pushed aside and dismissed. Especially by their own mother. And definitely not in front of the woman they're seeing.

"I'll come," she says as she unbuckles her seat belt. As she reaches for her purse on the floorboard, my mother's gaze finally finds its way over here.

A puff of smoke slowly billows from her mouth. Other than that, there's no reaction. I know she recognizes me though, because she doesn't look away. My chest tightens, making each breath more difficult. I focus on forcing air in and out. Just in and out.

The neighborhood is quiet when I step out, listening to the sound of Allie's door and then mine clunk close before I turn to look back at my mother. She's still seated, blowing out another puff before stubbing out her cigarette on the concrete step.

Allie waits for me before making her way across the street.

This was fucking stupid. It's all I can think as I make my way back to a house I hate, back to a woman I loathe. The anger is subdued, though. It's so messed up that even after all these years, I want something to change between the two of us.

That's the first mistake. Having hope.

"Dean?" my mother says and slowly stands up on the stoop. Her sweatpants hang loose on her body, as does the shirt she's wearing. I keep my shoulders square and look my mother in the eye.

"What are you here for?" she asks, setting her hands on her hips and narrowing her gaze.

I was right in my assumption from the car, she's lost

weight. Could be the cigarettes or it could be the stress of losing Rick. Maybe she's been like this for years. I don't know.

"I heard about Rick," I tell her and as I do, I feel Allie's small hand brush against mine, so I take it. It's funny how that little touch makes my heart hammer harder but in a way, it's calming.

My mother breaks eye contact and looks past me as I tell her I'm sorry for her loss.

"I'm sorry too," Allie says politely but in a voice that's genuine and full of pain.

"Yeah...well, thanks," my mother says coldly, dismissively.

"Mom," I say, and it feels odd calling her that, so I have to pause before continuing, "this is Allison. Allison, this is my mother."

I introduce them and Allie steps forward with her hand out to give my mother a handshake, even though she's still standing two steps higher than us.

True to form, my mom's a fucking bitch, leaving Allie hanging there with an empty hand held high. She looks at Allie good and hard before nodding her head and saying, "Hi."

The air turns frigid around me when I see Allie's face fall. Allie's innocent in all this. I shouldn't have brought her here.

Taking a large step forward, I shield Allie from my mother. "Just wanted to tell you that I'm doing fine, if you were wondering." My words come out hard and bitter. I don't know what the good doctor was thinking or what I was thinking when I decided to take his advice.

But there, I've told her, so we can get the fuck out of here.

"Fine? Is that what you call getting arrested?" My anger falters, even if just for a moment while my mother's face forms a twisted sneer. "I always knew you were no good."

I bite my tongue and hold back the explanation. She doesn't deserve one.

Just as I'm about to tell her goodbye forever, Allie steps around me, brushing against my leg as she shoves herself in front of me.

She's short, shorter than both me and my mom and she has to crane her neck to look in my mother's hard eyes as she tells her, "He was trying to do the right thing."

I haven't seen Allie angry really. I've seen her want to run, or pick a fight. But I've never seen her pissed like this. Her little hands fisted at her side. Her chin held high and her eyes narrowed. It's sweet of her, but I wish it weren't because of me.

"I'm sure," my mother says and then pulls out another cigarette. She lights it and adds, "If you're here for money, Rick didn't leave anything to you."

My body tightens and my heart feels like it's being squeezed. It fucking hurts. I can't deny it.

I don't know why what she said pains me even more. Not that Rick didn't give me anything, but that she'd think I'd come back here looking for a handout.

Then again, money's the only thing that ever mattered

to her.

"He's not going to do anything with his life, so you should really consider your other options," my mother tells Allie. She nods her head condescendingly as she speaks to Allie and doesn't even bother to look at me.

"What a bitch," Allie says with a high-pitched voice, looking my mother directly in the eye. "You didn't tell me she was this much of an asshole." She turns her head to look at me with disbelief and then seems to check her anger when I don't respond.

"Your son's a good man and I have no clue how he got lucky enough to get away from you."

My mother laughs. "Aww, sweetheart, I hope you enjoy getting your heart broken."

Allie opens her mouth again, and her face is scrunched up as she bites her tongue. She's letting my mother get the best of her.

The difference between these women is simple. Allie cares; my mother doesn't.

I wrap one arm around Allie's waist and pull her in close to me, letting her ass press against my upper thigh and cut her off.

"Like I said, just wanted to give you my condolences."

Allie peeks up at me with a bewildered look. "Let's go," I tell her softly, not bothering to tell my mother goodbye.

Chapter 23

Allison

"Are you angry with me?" I ask Dean and then try to swallow. But I can't. There's a spiked lump in the back of my throat that won't go away.

I know I'm a bitch. I'll be the first to admit it.

I like to hate people before they can hate me. I'll call them out, but I call myself out on my own shit. I know it doesn't make it right, though.

"I didn't mean to upset you when I called your mother a bitch... or an asshole. Whatever the hell I said to her." Even as I give him the apology, I feel awkward and like I've done him a disservice. He wanted to make things right with her and I think I just made things even worse. I don't even remember what all I said.

I fidget with my thumbs nervously as I wait for Dean to look at me. I feel awful. "I should have just been quiet," I tell him, and my voice cracks a little.

"You're fine," he says and lifts the turn signal lever, the ticks echoing in the hollow cabin of the car.

"What I said wasn't, though," I say. "I'm sorry, truly."

Dean softens. He's been tense and stiff ever since we left. My words have been caught in the back of my throat. It's weird feeling this overwhelming urge to be forgiven. I'm not used to it. At least not like this.

"I told you she's a bitch," he says as he straightens out the wheel and leans back, setting his hand on my thigh in that same spot as before. Moving his thumb in the way I like. I'm getting used to him doing that and even more, I'm growing to love the little touches. I cover his hand with mine and peek up at him.

"Next time, I'll be quiet."

He turns to look at me with a pinched expression. "There's not going to be a next time." My stomach sinks and I can't breathe until he adds, "I'm not going back there again."

"Well, if there's ever any other thing..." I stumble over my words. "I won't—"

"I like that you stood up for me," Dean says, cutting me off.

"You like it, so you forgive me? Or you like it—"

"I like the way you handled yourself. I'm not mad at all.

There's nothing to forgive."

"So we're okay?" I ask him desperately, my heart hurting more than it should and it's only just now that I realize what I really feel for Dean. This wasn't supposed to happen. Wiping under my eyes I close them and lean my head back against the seat, attempting to calm down.

Dean lets out a humorous breath which gets my attention, with a light in his eyes that eases me. "You're sweet, Allie Cat," he tells me and then gives me a soft smile.

"Where are we going?" I ask, finally relaxing back into the seat and sitting cross-legged. Again, pretending this is okay. He tries to take his hand away, but I put it right back on my thigh and he lets me. Right now I need him to keep from falling apart. I can figure out the rest tomorrow.

"The hotel around the corner has good room service," he says. "Or at least it used to."

"I like room service."

"And then you can tell me something to take my mind off the fact that I'm fucking stupid for coming down here at all."

"Why did you?" I ask him.

"Because my shrink said I should."

"Why?"

"My guess would be, so we could talk about our issues."

I let that sink in for a moment before I ask him, "Do you want to talk about them?"

He hesitates and takes his hand back, but only to steer

into a parking lot. It's not until he puts the car in park and turns it off before he answers. "Sometimes I think I do." With the hum of the engine and the stereo off, it's quiet. Too quiet.

"I'm here if you want to talk," I offer him although my stomach twists and that unsettled feeling comes back to me.

"I'd like to talk about something else," he says.

"About what?" I ask him, straightening my shoulders and preparing myself to talk about whatever he wants.

"I don't know," he says and I let out a small laugh. "How about your major?"

"Undecided."

"No shit? Me too." He gives me a handsome grin that settles those nerves and I reply, "Great minds, huh?"

"My lack of direction and commitment in choosing a major is one of the reasons Dr. Robinson said I should talk to my mother." He keeps tapping his thumb on the wheel and I'm not sure why he's so nervous.

He looks out the front windshield and toward the street as he talks. "Shit, I don't want to talk about that."

"You have no direction or commitment? Oh God, I really should hightail it out of here," I joke to lighten up the mood.

He chuckles, that deep, rough chuckle I love to hear and grabs my hand, pulling it to his lips. I love his smiles but I hate that he's only doing this to make me feel better. If I weren't here, he wouldn't be smiling. I know that much. "I like you,

Allie," he says softly and then adds, "I'm sorry I brought you and you had to see that."

In this moment, I'm drowning. I'm in over my head and the weight of everything pushes against my chest, forcing me farther down into an abyss that's sure to consume me.

But I want it to. Go ahead, swallow me whole.

When I look into Dean's eyes and see the emotion that stares back at me, I see myself and it hurts. It's a sweet, deep pain that I want to take from him. If that means drowning, so be it.

"Hey, you okay?" Dean asks me and it's only then I realize I wasn't breathing. That keeps happening around him.

"I'm just sorry," I croak out and Dean pulls me into his lap. It's odd with the wheel behind me but he's quick to push back his seat and I find myself tearing up. I haven't cried in years and I'm embarrassed.

"Shhh," Dean shushes me, and I hate myself. He's the one who has a right to be angry, to be upset, yet he's comforting me.

"I'm sorry," I say again, angrily wiping at my eyes and refusing to cry.

"It's okay," he whispers, petting my hair as the air hits my heated face.

"I don't know why I'm being like this." I wrap my arms around myself. It doesn't stop him from pulling me back against his chest and I instantly melt into his warmth.

"It doesn't matter, I'm here," he tells me and for the first time, it feels like those words carry weight. Like nothing else matters, as long as he's here.

I know it's not true but for a moment, it's nice to feel like it's real.

None of this was supposed to happen.

I wasn't supposed to fall for him.

Chapter 24

Deann

I knew she was breakable.

The moment I saw her, I fucking knew it.

She was hiding something and barely holding herself together, still is.

I could feel it in my bones.

After all this time, I still don't know what it is that's going to break her, though.

The door to the hotel room opens slowly with a creak and I have to glance over my shoulder to see if she's still with me. Her eyes are distant but she's there. She tucks a strand of her brunette hair behind her ear but it quickly falls back to where it was, and she doesn't bother with it again.

"Home sweet home," I say more to get her attention than anything else and push the door open wider. Her smile is weak but it's an offering I take.

"Thanks," she says as she walks in, hitching the strap of her duffle bag up her shoulder.

I grit my teeth. Even in this moment, with her little head messed up and something dark slowly consuming her, even now she won't let me hold her bag.

I walk in behind her, listening to the sound of my heart beating in rhythm with her soft breathing. As the door closes with a loud click, the air conditioner turns on and the curtains stir, making Allie jump.

She reaches up to her collarbone with her hand and then lets out a small laugh.

"You all right, Allie?" I ask her for the third time since we got out of the car. I already know the answer, even as she swallows thickly and lowers herself to the bed, all the while nodding. "Fine."

"You seem a little shaken," I tell her. "Something's bothering you."

"I'm fine," she says again with a sharp defiance in her voice.

The corners of my lips kick up. "And I'm the pope." I turn my back to her, picking up my bag to put it on top of the small dresser and unzip it but leave it there untouched.

"You're not thinking about running, are you?" I ask her, partly joking, partly serious.

"I'm just sorry, okay?" she says to my back and I turn to look at her, but I don't say anything.

She clears her throat and the soft lines of her bare neck get my attention as she talks. My eyes travel to the dip in her throat, then back to her lips.

"Sorry for getting all worked up," she clarifies.

"You can do what you want," I say while pulling the shirt over my head. It's hot as fuck in here and as I ball up my shirt I look for the thermostat, finding it on the other side of the room. She talks as I walk past her.

"Sure." As I dial down the temperature, she flops down on the bed, her legs still over the edge but her back flat on the mattress. "It doesn't mean I should, though," she whispers.

"I'm happy you let me in a little," I say and my chest pangs with pent-up emotion at the admission. Maybe it's pain, maybe it's gratitude. It's hard to tell the difference.

"You don't look so happy," she says.

"Is that why you're all upset?" I ask her, stopping at the edge of the bed and towering over her. Upset's not quite the right word but I don't know how to say it. "All because I'm pissed off that my mom is … the same she's always been." Again the air clicks on and her shoulders shake slightly from the noise.

"I'm not upset," she says but the words come out sounding more like a question, her eyes searching mine.

"Ever since we walked in here, you look like you've seen a ghost," I tell her. "Like you're on edge and waiting for something bad to happen." I stand my ground and the faint light from the sole window in the room casts a shadow of my form over Allison.

"Bad things always happen," she says after a moment of consideration. "Whether you wait for them or not."

"You look scared, Allie, and I don't like it."

"I am scared," she confesses in a hoarse whisper.

"I know my mother looks like shit, but I promise she's not as scary as she looks," I joke and she finally breaks a smile although the second she does, she closes her eyes and her face crumples. Goddamn, it hurts. It hurts to see her like this. It's even worse because I don't know how to make it better.

The bed groans, protesting as I sit on the edge and pull her small body into my arms. I don't talk as her shoulders shake. I just kiss her hair and rub her back.

Her body molds to mine for a small moment. A tiny but significant moment where she lets it out.

I'd swear she was crying if she didn't peek up at me with glossy eyes but not a tear leaving her. "I'm okay." She mouths the words more than speaking them and pulls away from me.

My fingertips brush over her shoulders and she catches my hand in hers as she sits cross-legged on the bed. "I just ..." She doesn't finish and shakes her head instead.

"Is it because of your mom?" I ask her. It's all I can think of. There wasn't a damn thing said that seemed to set her off. It was after the silence in the car and the time to think.

Sometimes our inner thoughts are our worst demons.

"No," she says with a sad smile and sniffles. She gives me a smile and even though the light in her eyes is dimmed, she almost looks normal. Like she can bandage up her pain and hide it. I suppose that's what she's used to and my body tenses as I debate what to do. Push her for more, not let her hide? Or just try to ease the pain and go along with this facade. I don't know what the hell to do, but I'm terrified she's going to push me away.

Her thumb brushes along the knuckles of my hand.

"I think I do want to text her, though," she says and swallows. The nervousness in her voice reflects in her eyes. She chews on her lower lip and searches my eyes again.

It looks like she's lying.

That's exactly what it looks like.

I don't know why or what's gotten to her, but she's fucking lying to me.

"You should," I say absently and let her hand fall as I walk back to the dresser. "Unless she's like my mom, in which case, fuck it."

"It took a lot for you to go to her."

I only nod at Allie's words. I don't look behind me as I slip into sweatpants even though I can hear her crawling on the bed.

"I would say I'm proud of you, but who am I to say that?" she says sarcastically. That protective armor of hers is sneaking up again.

"It makes me feel good that you're proud," I tell her bluntly.

Her gaze catches mine for a moment before she rubs the exhaustion from her eyes.

"I only did it because the shrink said to," I tell her.

"You still did it," she says softly, so soft I almost didn't hear but then she raises her voice to add, "It's hard to go through with things sometimes."

"Like what things?" I ask but she doesn't answer.

I wait a while, looking through the pile of binders on the nightstand until I find the one with the menu in it. She still hasn't answered, so I drop it.

"You want to split something?" I ask and she nods weakly.

"I'm not too hungry, but if you order fries I'll probably eat some ... or all of them." The small bit of humor forces the start of a smile on my face and I pick up the phone to place the order.

A burger with all the fixings and two orders of fries.

Hanging up the phone, I still don't feel right. I never thought bringing Allie out here would wind up like this. With me feeling A-fucking-okay and her looking like she's been beaten up.

"Thanks for coming with me," I tell her as she picks at something on the pajama pants she slipped on while I was ordering food. She lies on the bed, stretching out and tells me it's been a blast, again making the tense air lighter. She's good at that. Good at playing things off like they don't matter. Even now while she's breaking down right in front of me.

"Can I ask you something, Allie?" I say and then turn

around to see her texting something. She doesn't stop until she hits send and then looks up at me.

"Whatever you want." Before I can say another word, the screen of her phone lights up and pings. She tries to ignore it but on the second ping, she has to look down to silence her phone.

"I can wait," I say but she only shakes her head in response, tossing her phone onto the nightstand with a heavy breath and tired eyes.

Something is killing her inside. And it fucking hurts that she's hiding it from me still.

"What is it you wanted to ask?" she says with a soft and kind voice, one that begs for mercy. Our eyes lock and there's a shift between us. One of vulnerability. One seeking refuge in me.

"I just don't want you to ever lie to me." I don't know why that's what comes out. But it's all I've got for her. "You don't have to tell me shit," I begin but pause when her expression falls and she fails to hide the sadness there. "You don't have to tell me shit, but don't lie to me."

She nods once and then agrees in a small voice, "That's not really a question but ... No lying. Can do."

"You all right?"

"Yeah," she says but doesn't look me in the eyes as she pulls the covers back.

"And that's the truth?" I ask her, reminding her of the assurance she just made.

"As all right as I can be," she says and then slowly raises

her eyes to mine. "Just a lot of things happened when I was younger, and something reminded me of a promise I made but almost broke."

"What promise?"

"Can we just eat and go to sleep?" she asks in return and chances a quick glance at me, again picking at some nonexistent fuzz on her pants.

"It's not that late," I tell her out of impulse. It can't be any later than nine.

"How about we just cuddle and watch something funny?" she asks, and her voice is stronger, more hopeful.

"A comedy? I'm always down for that."

Crawling into bed beside her feels right. Like that's what I'm supposed to do right now. Before I even have a chance to wrap my arm around her waist and pull her into me, she's already nestling her ass into my crotch and getting comfortable.

She reaches behind her, looking back at me and takes the remote off the nightstand. Before getting back into position she gives me a quick peck and then picks up my hand in both of hers.

"Your hands are so small," I say absently as she traces the lines on my hand with the tip of her finger. It's soothing and gentle, but it stops when she kisses the tips of my fingers like I did with hers.

"I wish things were different," she whispers. There's a sincerity there, a fear too.

"Like what? My mom?"

She shakes her head and settles her back against me, letting my hand fall to her waist.

"Just circumstances," she says without looking back.

With the remote in hand, she searches the channels while I watch her. The light from the television brightens her face.

I see every detail. There are moments in time that don't seem like they mean anything at all when they happen. Moments that hold no significance at the time.

But later, those moments are burned into your memory.

The way the light hits her hair, the way she blinks away the tears that threaten to fall. The way she smiles up at me with the sound of some movie playing on the television in the background. Some moments are burned into your memory forever, and maybe it's because deep inside we wish it could stay like this. With her nestled in my arms, knowing she's safe and that nothing bad is going to happen tonight.

There are times in life when you run toward something.

And there are times you run away.

Neither choice is shameful.

But either way, you're running.

CHAPTER 25

ALLISON

"Sam?" I call out her name again and my voice echoes in the empty hallway.

There's no one else around. The deserted halls of the school mock me as I move from room to room looking for her. "Sam," I barely whisper her name.

It feels odd as I open the doors. Almost like they're expecting me, since they open so easily. They creak open slowly though, making me wait as I hold my breath.

Each room gives me nothing. They're all empty and dark and every time it scares me to move beyond the doorframe. So, I just look in and whisper her name. Quietly, praying she'll hear me.

Door after door, I keep moving through the hall. Waiting

to see her. I can picture how she used to sit on top of her desk, cross-legged with her book in her lap. I keep waiting to see her there smiling back at me. But there's nothing. Just empty rooms, each one darker than the next. The halls grow cold and I forget why I need her.

I thought I was following her. I swear I heard her call for me.

She needs my help. The reminder makes my body freeze as a chill flows over me and makes the hairs on the back of my neck stand up. I can feel it. Deep down in my gut, the pain twists and turns, writhing into a coil that crawls up my spine.

She needs me, and I'm failing her.

The last door opens before I touch the knob. The light flickers on and off and then settles dimly in the center of the room. On Sam. But she's not seated on the desk. She's slumped against the wall, sitting on the floor by the closed, dark window.

Her eyes are sad and her face hollowed.

The darkness around her makes her seem pale and colorless.

"I'm sorry," she whispers.

My body jolts upright as the silent scream tears through me.

My heart races and sweat covers my body. I can hardly hear Dean as he grips me harder, staring at me and pushing the hair out of my face. I can't see or hear anything other than Sam.

It was like I was really there.

Like she was right there.

"Allison," Dean says, his voice piercing through the memory. "Are you okay?"

He's breathless, his fingers digging into my shoulder and his dark gaze pinning me in place. It takes me a long second before I realize he's here with me. He's here now. His palm brushes against my forehead again, pushing the loose strands of hair away from my face. He's so warm and my body's freezing.

I blink away the vision of the night terror and try desperately to calm my breathing as his hold loosens and I bring the covers up closer to my neck.

Her voice was so clear.

My breathing won't calm. My chest heaves violently as I wipe my eyes and pull away from him. She was right there. Sam was right there.

"Talk to me," Dean commands me but that's just not possible.

Slowly, my heart calms.

"You were having a nightmare," Dean tells me like I don't know what happened. "It was just a nightmare."

My head nods of its own accord as I slip back beneath the covers, seeking their warmth.

I can still feel the cold metal of the doorknob.

"Sometimes I have bad dreams," I tell Dean. To stop his questioning.

"About what?"

The words slip from me immediately. "I don't want to talk about it."

I haven't had a dream like that in a long damn time.

I haven't fallen asleep so easily in just as long.

"Are you okay?"

He's asked me that so many times in the last twelve hours.

"I'm fine," I say. "I'm sorry."

"Don't be sorry," he tells me and it's only then that his expression comes into focus.

My heart melts, slowly but with a heat that's undeniable. "I just want to make sure you're all right," he says as he brushes my hair from my face. In this moment, I'm weak with want for him and his touch.

I didn't know until this day what I'd do for him and how much he meant to me.

Maybe that's why she came back to remind me.

To remind me of the promise I made to her and why I'm here.

"I'm fine," I tell him. I know it's a lie when I say it. A lie and a broken promise I've only just made. I should feel guilty. But I don't. The other promise is more important.

I don't feel guilty while I cup his cheek in my hand and brush my lips against his.

Not while I let him hold me.

Not even as he whispers he loves me into my hair when he thinks I've fallen asleep. And that's what it is. Love. I feel it too. I'm not blind to it. I even accept it although I can't have it. I can't have Dean. This has gone on for far too long.

It's not okay to be okay.

That would be the worst tragedy.

Chapter 26

Dean

"Bottoms up!" Kev says over the sound of the music echoing off the walls of the room. The bass pounds through my veins as I toss the shot back. Partially to let go, partially out of anger.

Allison fucking ghosted. Hasn't been to her classes, isn't returning my texts. The second we got back here, she left me high and dry.

My fist clenches around the empty shot glass as the whiskey burns down my throat.

I should have known better than to pretend she was fine. I should have seen this shit coming.

"Ahh," James hisses as he shakes his head, slamming the

glass down on the coffee table. His face is scrunched even as he yells out, "Whoo!" as if he's having the fucking time of his life.

And maybe the other assholes here are. As each glass hits the table, everyone around me seems lighter, happier, ready to party. That's what this is. A party.

The air from my lungs leaves me as Kev's hand pounds on my back.

"You my wingman tonight?" he asks me, lowering his face to mine as I hunch over the countertop. I follow his gaze to the set of brunettes across the room.

One with short hair and a bright pink tank top, while the other has her long hair pulled back and is wearing a short little black dress. They laugh as they spot Kev staring them down like they're prey. They're nothing like Allie. Kev can have them both. He nods and they blush, covering their faces with the red plastic cups of beer in their hands.

"Not tonight," I finally answer. I'm not feeling it. There's only one girl I want to see here, and I know for a fact she knows I'm here. She knows where to find me. She's not here because she doesn't want me. I'm not stupid and her hints aren't subtle.

I went to her place, but she didn't answer.

She's pissing me off more than anything. With the whiskey flowing through my veins, there's not much of anything keeping me from going back to her house right now.

"Why the fuck not?" he asks me, rearing his head back to

look at me like I'm being unreasonable.

"Not tonight," I repeat and toss the plastic shot glass into the trash. That was the third or fourth shot I've had over the course of fifteen minutes. Maybe fifth. One after the other and I sway slightly, but the cup makes it into the bin.

"Is it that chick?" he asks. *That chick.* That's not her name.

"Yeah," I tell him and my body feels tight, even as my vision tilts. She's fucking with me and she knows it. Worst of all, I'm letting her.

"Suit yourself," he says as he fills a cup from the tap of the keg.

Anger rises in a slow billow as I watch the foam rise to the top of the rim.

"What the fuck does that mean?" The words slip from me without any deliberate intention. It's the anger taking over. Not at him. It's anger directed at her.

"Calm down," Kev tells me, scrunching his brow and looking over his drink at me. "I didn't mean shit."

James laughs and it pisses me off. The room tilts in the opposite direction when I look at him.

"You got something to say?" I ask him. Because the fucker looks like he has something to say. The second the question leaves me, the front door opens and there she is.

The short dress hits her upper thigh as she kicks the door shut, letting the thin fabric swirl around her. From head to toe, she has every detail in place. From her straightened hair to the high heels that complement the bracelets adorning her wrist.

That devilish smile isn't in sight as she turns toward the kitchen, toward us, and instantly catches my gaze. Like she could feel me watching her. I take her in slowly, feeling like an asshole for thinking she was avoiding me.

She wouldn't have come if she didn't want me. Right?

But then her eyes flash and she rips her gaze away.

She came to end it.

My heart slams once, then twice, as she stalks toward us. In my blurred periphery, I see James lean in closer and say quietly but with an arrogance I'm not in the mood for, "That's the type of girl who fucks you raw when you show up to her house. Lets you fuck her in public. Likes to flirt. Likes attention. And will do anything to get it. Or anyone." He nods his head as he talks, staring at something behind me. My knuckles turn white as the anger builds in response to his oblivious nature. "You really want to be tied up with that?" he asks me and my head turns slowly. So fucking slowly and against my will as Allison heads right for us.

"Watch your fucking mouth." My words come out sharp and as I turn toward him, everyone else takes a step back.

The heat rises and my shoulders feel tense.

James looks at me like a deer in fucking headlights. Like he didn't see it coming. Like those weren't fighting words that just came out of his mouth.

Before I can say a damn thing, I feel a strong arm push me

back slightly, making me face Allison and not that asshole.

"Look who's in the house," Daniel says, wrapping his arm tighter around my shoulder and inserting himself between me and James. He keeps a strong grip on me and whispers for me to calm down. That she's here and everything's fine. That it's not worth it. And that last line is what repeats itself as Allie comes closer, looking between all of us like she wishes she hadn't come. *That it's not worth it.*

The fuck it isn't.

I struggle to know what to do. The whiskey and the anger swirl into a deadly concoction in the pit of my stomach.

I'm a fucking mess. Daniel's good-natured laugh seems at odds with what's flowing in my veins.

But he's different from me. Daniel has a way of smiling through the bullshit. Of acting like things don't bother him, when inside he's envisioning slitting your throat. It's how he was raised.

"What's up, sweetheart?" he asks Allie as she glances from James to him, then to me before setting her purse down on the counter.

The metal links of the strap clink as they hit one another, and I force myself to focus on that, rather than the sound of James leaving the kitchen.

My teeth and fists are still clenched, the skin pulled taut over my knuckles.

"You tell me, *sweetheart*," she says, mocking Daniel but

her confidence is barely there, and her focus is split between us and watching James's back.

"Shot?" Daniel asks as the music plays the word over and over. *Another round of shots.*

Her eyes flicker from me to him and as she parts her lips to respond, I interject. "Come on," I tell her, grabbing her wrist and shrugging Daniel off of me.

He hovers for a moment as she stares back at me, ripping her arm away.

The tension grows and the air goes still and quiet; even the fucking music seems to dim as she considers whether or not to listen to me.

Shit, I guess it doesn't matter either way.

I can see it written on her face. She's running. From me and what we had. She only came here to tell me as much. Least she could do is to not say it in front of them.

"Lead the way, Neanderthal," she says sarcastically, avoiding Daniel's piercing gaze. Like he's her fucking protector. I can see it. He's watching the two of us like he knows shit's about to go down. Judging by the way everyone averts their gaze when I look at them, he's not the only one thinking that.

I ignore him as much as she does and lead her to the door, not really touching her, just staying close as we walk outside.

The music dies the second the door shuts and the sticky heat of the late summer air and faint sounds of crickets from the woods behind us surround us.

I could use a drag. It's been ages since I've had a smoke but right now, I'm hit hard with the need for a cigarette.

"What's wrong with you?" Allie asks me the moment she turns on her heels to face me.

"Where have you been?" I question her in return. "We came back Sunday. You missed two classes, texted me back with one-word answers and have been blowing me off." I pace on the small cement landing in front of the door. "I mean, I knew shit was off on the way home, but all I asked from you was for you to be honest."

"What wasn't honest?" Allie bites back with anger. Good. I hope she's pissed like I am.

"You don't have to lie to be dishonest," I say and even in my drunken stupor, I know that those words make more sense than any excuse she can come up with.

"Yeah, well, I wanted to tell you something anyway," she starts and I scoff at her.

"I gave you the fucking over you needed, huh?"

She shakes her head, that gorgeous hair of hers swirling around her shoulders as the heat climbs and I run a hand through my hair. No matter how put together she is, her eyes can't lie to me. She can look pissed or like she doesn't care. But her eyes have the same sad look in them they did at the hotel.

"What are you talking about?" Exasperation is clear in her voice.

"You want to be with me or not, Allie?" I ask her the only question I need an answer to and her plump lips part slightly, the immediate answer begging to slip from them, but she stops herself, slamming her mouth shut and swallowing the words.

"I knew it," I tell her and feel pathetic. I'm not the pathetic one, though. This is on her. She's the one running from this. She's the one who's scared.

"It's not you," she says with way too little emotion in her voice. Like it doesn't even matter.

"Oh, it's not me, it's you?" I ask with a bitter taste in my mouth. "Is that what you're going for? Really? You can be more creative than that." She flinches at the anger in my voice. "Come on Allie, I'll give you a minute to come up with something better," I sneer and lean into her. I'm pissed. I'm so fucking pissed.

It's easier than being hurt.

Everyone pushes me away because they don't want me. She wants me. I know she does. And still, I can't hold on to her.

"How about the fact that you were ready to get into a goddamn brawl when I walked in. How about that?"

"How about it?" I ask back. I don't remember quite what happened or what she knows. All I remember is that someone said something that they deserved to be punched for. I don't tell her that though, I stand there like an ass, waiting for her to fill me in on what the hell happened.

I shouldn't have drunk so much. If I'd known she was

coming, I wouldn't have.

"I don't need you to stick up for me," she says and James's stupid fucking face flashes in my head.

"It's not about sticking up for you. You're *mine*." I thump my hand against my chest to emphasize my words.

"I'm not yours. I don't belong to anyone!" she screams at me and takes a step closer. The heat from the argument is at odds with the chill in the night air.

"Knock it off," I tell her. "You know what I mean."

"This is why I can't ..." she starts to say, but even she can't hold on to the thin excuse.

"Quit pushing people away—quit hiding," I beg her through clenched teeth.

"How am I the one who's hiding?"

"You just need a reminder of who you belong to, don't you?" I ask her and take a step forward, closing the space between us. She's so close. So small and all I want to do is pick her ass up and show her she's mine. I can remind her. She just needs my touch.

"You're drunk," Allie says in a harsh whisper and looks behind me at the door to the frat house. I watch the hollow of her throat as she swallows thickly, and something flashes in her eyes.

"Would that make it better or worse?" I ask her and imagine taking her right here, right now. "If I fucked you right there in the dirt," I offer her.

"Dean, don't," she whimpers and closes her eyes, wrapping her arms around her shoulders. Like it hurt her. "Please," she begs me and it's like a slap in the face.

"Please what?" I ask her calmly, trying to pull my shit together. "I didn't mean to ..." Hurt her. I didn't mean to put that look on her face.

"Allie Cat," I speak softly, reaching up to hold her shoulders and pull her in closer, but she takes a step back. Her heels clack on the landing.

"I don't want this," she finally says and it's then I see the tears. Real tears, flowing freely and she doesn't brush them away. It stuns me for a second.

"Please, you're drunk and this, what's between us, it's over."

"Why?" I expect anger, but this feeling in my chest isn't that. "Just tell me why. I'll fix it."

I swear I can fix it. I can change. For her, I will.

"You don't commit to a goddamn thing," she says out of nowhere. Like she finally remembered the made-up excuse she could use.

"I committed to you!" The words come out loud and leave me hollow and empty. "I love you!" I yell the words although I don't mean to. So loud, the words burn on their way up. I fucking love her. My heartbeat slows and the anger leaves in a slow wave at the realization. It's been a long damn time since I've felt loved by someone, but I know she loves me back. Whether she says it or not. Somewhere in there she does. But she doesn't want to and that's what's different about us.

"Well, that was your first mistake," she says and waits. I stand there, letting everything hit me. What I feel, what she feels. When she turns around and the rapid pace of her heels echoes through the air, I feel numb.

Not because of what she said, I knew it was coming.

It's because even feeling all this for her and knowing I love her, and that she loves me, it's not enough.

Even with all that being true, she won't stay with me. And I don't know why.

Chapter 27

Allison

I don't know why I can't stop crying.

It's not just little hiccups and occasional outbursts when you least expect it. It's the violent sobs that refuse to leave. The kind of crying that hurts your chest to the point where you're in physical pain. The kind that makes you curl up and huddle in the middle of the floor with only a throw blanket as if it will save you.

But nothing can. Because the pain is from the inside.

This isn't me. Dean broke me. He flipped a switch somewhere deep within me and I can't find it. I can't flick the damn thing back to where it's supposed to be.

There's not a part left remaining of the girl I set out to be.

This isn't what I planned.

Right now, all I want is him. I want to take it all back.

I want to be someone else. It's not fair that these are the cards I was dealt. Or maybe I'm just an idiot for how I played them.

I pull the blue plaid throw tighter around my shoulders as a shiver runs through me. There's a pile of used tissues next to me and I hate them. They're evidence that I'm losing myself. Or maybe I've just been hiding all along.

The thought makes my spine prickle with yet another freezing bite.

It's cold.

Loneliness is cold.

Regret is even colder.

As I sit in the empty house, eerily quiet and waiting for the next bout of bullshit tears to consume me, I try to think of which part of all this I regret the most. Or maybe, a more difficult question to answer: at what point did I start to feel regret?

My body jolts when the phone in my hand pings.

I have several messages from my mother to read still. I can't bring myself to look right now. I'm so weak I'd tell her everything.

I can feel the confession on the tip of my tongue. The last time I confessed to her, it ruined me and turned me hateful. I can't make that mistake again.

I need to tell someone.

The words are so close to escaping, I almost told Angie. A

girl I don't even know. Simply because she was there to listen.

She spoiled it, though. I could feel the weight lifting off my shoulders before I even let the truth escape. Class was over, Dean never showed, and the emptiness inside me brewed to a boil. Even though it was perfect. *This is perfect.*

"I think it's best to stay away from guys like that," she told me.

And that's what made me keep quiet.

What kept the words deep down inside.

What if I didn't want to stay away?

What if I knew what I was doing?

She wouldn't understand and she'd be disgusted with me if I told her what I really wanted. More than anything else. But it's our secret. Our promise. They won't know why.

My phone pings again and my body shudders. I'm quick to place it on silent but then the thought of missing a text from Dean makes me change it back.

Pathetic.

I'm so fucking pathetic. Clinging to the idea of what could be.

As if it would even be possible for someone like me.

Someone so consumed with destruction.

I glance at the texts from my mom.

The first line is from me to her.

Only an apology, and a vague one at that.

I'm sorry, I told her. I couldn't not say it. Not while I sat in that hotel room wishing she were with me. Wishing I could take it all back. If only it were so easy to pluck words from the air and tuck them into your back pocket.

The series of texts from my mother hasn't stopped since then.

I think she thought I'd killed myself until I told her I hadn't.

I'm sorry for running. I sent her that text to explain, but it's not much of an explanation at all. I can't tell her the truth though because I'm still running, and she'll stop me.

Just like Dean would.

They can't stop this from happening. My body stiffens when I see my mother's last text.

I'm coming to see you.

I start to respond, but what can I say? *No, don't.* It's not like she'll listen.

When I delete it without hitting send, another text from her comes through.

You won't talk to me and this has to stop.

What has to stop? I text back.

I know that will make her drop it. Because she can't admit what happened. She can't apologize to me for what she did. She can't speak the truth.

I miss you, she finally answers me.

I wonder which version of me she misses. Probably the younger version. The one that isn't so fucked in the head.

I miss the old me too. But she's long dead and has been for years.

Chapter 28

Dean

The beer is cold and the head of it foams just right. It looks like a picture for a beer ad as it sits on the walnut bar of the Iron Heart Brewery on Lincoln and Church.

My back's to the door as I sit at the far end of the bar, closest to the large glass window. More people walk into the already crowded place, but I don't pay any attention to the chatter. I only stare out the window at the parking lot across the street.

"You want something else?" the bartender asks me and when I look up at him, interrupting whatever thought was in my head, he nods to the untouched beer.

"Nah, I'm good," I tell him and take a swig. Maybe I should ask for something stronger. Maybe I shouldn't drink at all. I don't know. I don't know shit and that's all I know for sure.

"All the way out here?" a voice too close for comfort asks and I turn around to see Daniel sliding onto the barstool next to me.

"I'll have what he's having," he tells the bartender and then squares his shoulders forward and squints like he's looking up at the menu.

"Some funny names for beer," he says absently.

"All local drafts," I tell him.

"Is that why you came all the way out here?" he asks me and I turn my gaze back to my beer and then take another long pull. I'm here because it's right around the corner from Dr. Robinson's office. I'm here because it's easy. The beer's good, the vibe is right, and everyone here leaves me the hell alone.

"How'd you find me?" I ask him and he shrugs.

"Been barhopping," he says like it's a coincidence. I huff in disbelief but I don't push him. Daniel's background isn't exactly sparkling clean.

He slaps down a few five-dollar bills as his beer hits the bar and then he finally faces me.

"She really messed you up that bad?" *Going right in for the kill.*

"I don't want to talk about it," I answer him simply, returning my gaze to the cracked concrete sidewalk across the street. A few people walk by and no one seems to notice it.

"Fair enough," he says with a nod and then asks for a menu.

"You're making yourself right at home, aren't you?"

"I've got to eat."

I take a good hard look at him as he opens the menu and pretends like this is some casual meetup.

"You don't have anything better to do?" I ask him and his dark gaze meets mine. There's a challenge in his eyes but one he lets go of quickly.

"Nothing I feel like doing right now."

Another moment passes and he closes the menu and pushes it forward, glancing over his shoulder to check out the game.

"What would you do?" I finally ask him. "If you were me?"

"If I wanted a girl, but she didn't want me?" he asks like that's what happened.

"She wants me," I tell him confidently and he huffs a sarcastic laugh. "She's scared," I tell him in a raised voice I didn't intend.

"Scared of you?" he asks like it's a valid question and I can't believe he'd say that.

"You think I'd hurt her?" My hackles raise, my muscles coiling. "I'd never give her a reason to fear me. I wouldn't hurt a woman."

"You're the one who said she's scared," he answers me and I let the anger wane, listening to the murmur of talking around us and the sounds of the football game on the screen as I think about how to explain my Allie Cat.

"What's she afraid of then?" Daniel asks me before I can tell him anything and I just shrug.

"What are we all afraid of?" I shoot back and then snort like I'm some fucking philosopher.

"Getting hurt ... or maybe that we'll be the ones to do the hurting," Daniel answers with nothing but sincerity. My throat tightens and I struggle to release my breath as I take in the weight of what he said.

I nod and chug my beer, drinking it all down. It hits the bar with a loud ring from the empty glass and I signal for another.

"Sometimes people hurt the ones who get close to them."

"I didn't hurt her," I say without looking away from the bar. I watch the bartender fill the glass, the beer spilling over before he wipes it off.

"I wasn't talking about you doing the hurting. Seems like she's the one who's got you on a leash."

I smirk at him and grab the beer with both hands.

"Maybe I like the leash," I joke and he finally breaks into a smile, but it's gone when he opens his mouth next.

"You like her doing that, though?" he asks. "Leading you on like that?"

"It's not what it looks like," I tell him and he's quick to respond with, "That's what they all say."

"I'm telling you, Allie feels something for me. There's something real there."

"But she's scared?" he asks like I'm being ridiculous. Without waiting for me to try to explain more, he continues.

"You can't make someone commit to you." His voice

turns bitter as he adds, "You can't make them want you." I'm struck by his words and the force of them until I realize he's talking about something else. *Someone else.*

"If she'd just tell me what the hell got to her, I'd make it right."

"Did you ask?"

The world seems to still at his question. The obvious answer is yes. I didn't, though, not really. I backed off. I didn't push her like I thought about doing. I could have pushed. I should have. I was so close, and I didn't do it.

"I didn't want to scare her off," I say and the words are a murmur.

"Instead you lost her," he says back and I stare at him like he's the asshole here. He shrugs and takes another sip of his beer before telling me, "Sometimes they come back, and sometimes you just have to go get them."

Chapter 29

Allison

There's something about these pajamas.

They remind me of Sam. She always wore pajamas, even to school. Blue and flannel with a tank top underneath, the pants folded over at the waist. A small smile graces my lips as I grab the bottle of Cabernet from the fridge.

That's how I want to remember her.

It's been five years, and only recently have I started to remember her like that. Back when she was the Sam I knew and loved. Back when we were best friends for life.

She wore pajamas like this when she was happy.

Not me, though. My heart sinks as I glance at my phone, sitting on the countertop of the small kitchen.

I think that was the final straw. Dean will never want me again.

That should make me happy, considering what my only goal is. The one thing I've wanted for so long. This arrangement is the best scenario. Available. Vulnerable. And the reputation of a slut. *Easy.* It would be all too easy.

As I pour the mostly empty bottle into the glass, I wonder if I'm crazy. The plan was crazy from the beginning, certainly not something a sane person would do. I knew that.

Then again, not many people would remain sane after seeing what I saw and knowing what I know.

Tragedies happen, but usually there's justice. A villain you can blame and prosecute.

When the villain gets off scot-free and destroys your life forever, that does something to a person. When he walks away unscathed and blends into a crowd that looks back at you like you're the one who's in the wrong.

It's even worse when you played a part in the wreckage and the small pieces that were shattered turn to ashes in your hands. You'll make all sorts of promises then. Promises to make wrongs right. At any cost.

"Whatever it takes," I whisper and lift the wine to my lips, drinking it in large gulps.

I barely taste it although the sweetness turns bitter quickly as it sits on my tongue.

It's a good thing I pushed Dean away, I think. *He deserves so much better.*

The bottle clinks and the sound resonates in the kitchen as I set it down. There wasn't even enough left to fill the glass.

One hand holds the wine, while the other picks up my phone.

I will him to text me, but nothing happens.

Slipping onto the stool, I lay my cheek down on the cold granite and stare at my phone. I scroll through our messages; I even laugh once or twice, even though it's a sad sound. These texts are proof that at one point I was happy.

I'm sorry. I text him, unable to keep myself from doing it. I'm sorrier than he'll ever know.

I glance around this place and hate that I'm even here. The sickness that's been in the bottom of my gut for so long begins to creep up.

I don't want to be here anymore. I don't want to do this.

It all hurts too much. *But I'm so close to the edge.* If only I can just hold on.

I'm so close to keeping a promise I never thought I could.

I drown my self-pity in the wine, throwing it back and trying to block out the images that keep coming back to me, but I have to stop when I hear a loud knock at the door. My eyes fly to the screen of my phone, the message marked as read.

Dean.

My feet trip over one another and I nearly fall in my desperation to get to the door. I'll tell him. I'll confess and he'll save me. God help me please, because I don't know what to do anymore.

With a racing heart and nearly breathless, I whip open the front door, not bothering to check to see who it is.

It's not Dean and my heart slows, as does time.

I guess this was what he needed. It's what he was waiting for.

A weakness leading to a way in.

I knew I was close to the edge, but I wasn't ready to jump. I guess I would never have jumped, though; it was all about being pushed.

I swallow the lump growing in my throat. "Kevin." I say his name out loud. This is the second time I've talked to him. Other than that night six years ago at Mike's house. I thought it would have taken more to lure him in. I didn't even try yet. I was still setting up the dominoes.

"What are you doing here?" I ask him, trying to hide the swell of anger ... and fear. My knuckles turn white as I grip the doorknob harder. "How did you know my address?" I ask him as it registers that I never told him. I'd planned on it, of course. My heart beats harder as I think about how this is exactly what I wanted. But not right now. Not like this.

I can barely breathe as he tells me, "I saw you walk home the other night from the frat house. It's not too far away."

It's not. I rented this place just for that reason. I didn't realize he'd noticed. I thought I'd have to tell him.

"I was just dropping by to check on you," he says and then

looks to his right and left. "You alone?" he asks.

I don't want to tell him I am but I nod once regardless. That's what a good victim would do. The perfect victim for him.

This is what I came here for. The entire reason I came to this town, this university.

The sole reason for my existence for the last six months. As soon as Grandmom died and there was nothing left to live for anymore.

To make him pay for what he did to her.

Even if I set him up, if the justice served is for what he does to me right now, it'll be worth it. She deserves to have him pay for what he is.

"Do you want to come in?" I ask him and I let my body sway slightly, thinking of Sam and how she needed this. I have a glass of wine in me, only one but I play up the drunkenness. Maybe that will make this happen quicker.

He doesn't answer me but he looks over his shoulder before coming in and shutting the door.

"You drinking?" he asks me, looking pointedly at the glass still in my hand. The dark liquid swirls as I shrug and try to think of what to say.

To think of what's happening right now and not the night that he crept into the bedroom where Sam was. I try not to think of what he did to her and what he's about to do to me. I was right there. So close to saving her. So close to preventing all this.

But I can make it all better now. I can make it right.

I can be his next victim and make him pay. Because that's what I came here to do.

"Dean doesn't want me anymore, so I thought I'd celebrate being single again," I say to the ground, keeping my eyes half-shut. I think maybe he'll use that to convince me to talk to him. Or to somehow try to weasel his way into me sleeping with him for revenge or something.

Whatever it takes.

"Already a bottle in?" he says with a smirk, looking at the empty bottle on the dining room table as he reaches for the buckle on his belt.

"What are you doing?" I ask out of instinct. My hair stands on end and my blood slows, my heart stops.

"I know how to make you feel better," he says as he pulls the leather through the loops of his pants. *Say something.* Two different voices scream in my head. One to let him, to agree with him. One to tell him no.

My blood runs cold. *Say something.* The need to run almost overwhelms me but I stand still. It's only when he drops the belt on the ground and lets the buckle clang that I can't hold it back any longer.

I don't want to tell him no because I want him to hurt me. This is exactly what I planned but I can't do it. I can't keep my promise to her.

"You should—"

"Come here," he interrupts me before I can say go.

I try to push him off of me, hating how he grips my arm. His thick fingers dig into my skin, bruising me and holding me still.

I didn't expect this. She was on the bed. She could barely move. She told me. But this isn't like that.

A scream tears from my throat and I try to run but he trips me, grabbing my thigh and covering my mouth.

"We both know you wanted this," he grunts as he digs into the waistband of my pajama pants.

He has no idea.

This is all I've wanted for so long.

For justice, the only way I know how to get it.

Even so, when he pushes me back against the sofa, I continue to fight him. At first, I think it's instinct. But when he smiles and grips my hips, pushing me and pulling me down, the sick feeling of regret makes my skin go cold.

"Leave me alone," I yell, scorching my throat but he doesn't listen. My nails rake the back of his hand as he shoves me down with a bruising force.

I wish I could stop him.

"Stop!" I scream out, kicking him, but he covers my face. My heart beats wildly.

I changed my mind. I don't want this. I try to scream again but he yanks my arm behind my back and pins me in place, forcing me facedown on the sofa.

"I've always wanted to play with a girl like you."

I'll never forget the smell of the blood. The air was thick with it although I didn't know what it was until later.

The floor creaked as I stepped into Sam's bedroom. I called out her name, pushing the door open wider, but deep down I already knew something had happened. The house was quiet, save the click of the air conditioner turning on. Even that made me jump.

Sam! I called out louder when I didn't see her on her bed where she usually was. Her phone was there, though. Right in the center of the neatly made bed.

I can still see her now, sitting cross-legged and bobbing her head, making her ponytail swish back and forth as she listened to the music blaring from her earbuds. But that was the old Sam. The girl who knew who she was and loved herself.

That was before she was raped. Before she was told it was her fault. That she should have known better. Before everyone looked at her like she was the only one to blame.

Before she believed that she'd genuinely deserved it. That there was something innately wrong with her. That she really had it coming to her. That's what everyone told her, so why would she think any different? Even if she didn't want it, it was because of what she'd done that he hurt her. And she was the one who was the problem.

I tried to call out her name again but my voice was hoarse as I saw the light filtering through the crack of the open bathroom door. And the note on the floor.

I'm sorry.
I'm sorry I ended it.
I'm sorry I went to the party.
I'm sorry I kissed those boys and led them on.
I'm sorry I drank. I'm sorry I ever talked to Kevin.
It hurt when he held me down.
I promise I tried to scream. I'm sorry you didn't hear me.
I'm sorry I didn't tell you sooner, Mom.
I'm sorry all of this happened.
I don't want to be this person.
I swear to you I'm sorry.

The world made her blind. She wasn't supposed to be sorry. Victims aren't the ones who are supposed to be sorry. I walked away unscathed, but Sam wasn't so lucky. She didn't hear my voice telling her that she wasn't a bad person because everyone else spoke in unison. She asked for it. What did she think would happen?

What did they think would happen when she was gone and only I was left, knowing her truth?

The paper crinkled in my hand. I'll never forget how neat

her penmanship was. How even with her last words, she made sure they were pretty and that she'd written each letter as best as she could.

My thumb traced over the one spot on the sheet of paper that was crinkled and slightly discolored. Where she'd let her tears fall onto the paper.

I don't know how I forced myself to move. Every step to the bathroom made my fear more real, made my skin that much colder.

My hand shook as I pushed open the bathroom door wider, my heart refusing to continue beating when I saw her.

Sam never cried before that night.

And she never smiled after it either.

"Sam," I said, and my voice scratched my throat as I fell to my knees in the bathroom. The tile was cold and hard. She was in the tub with the drain open and the water barely running. It mixed with the blood and pooled around her body.

Her pajama pants were stuck to her legs, soaking wet and stained with the blood.

I covered my mouth as I cried, hating the sight before me. After she slit her throat, she must have lurched forward; blood was splattered on the wall and on her arms. Like maybe she tried to stop it. But the knife lay by her thigh and she was still.

"Sam." I could barely say her name as I inched forward.

I had to touch her, even with her eyes open and staring back at nothing, a stillness that only comes with death. Even then I still had to climb into the tub and hold her, begging her to wake up.

But she never would.

Even as a fifteen-year-old girl, I knew that.

She hated herself for what she'd done. She came to believe she deserved it because that's what everyone told her. She was confused and she forgot how to be happy. She must've thought she never would be again and maybe she was right.

Worst of all, I left her.

I listened to my mother and left her when she needed me most. It could have been me and I didn't even stand beside her.

I could never take that back. But I made her a promise that night.

Chapter 30

Dean

There's an expression about seeing red.

They say when you're consumed with rage, you see red. Your sense of awareness is skewed. Your thoughts aren't logical. Your decisions aren't sane.

You're seeing red.

I've been angry before. I've let it get the best of me rather than accepting the pain that was always there.

I never knew the true meaning of seeing red until I heard Allie scream.

I could hear her behind the door.

I thought I heard her all the way from the sidewalk. It was a scream that made the hairs on my arm stand on end. A scream the neighbor heard as well and I caught her looking toward Allie's door with concern.

My heartbeat picked up and it was already pounding in my chest.

Every step I took before I heard her, I thought about the text I sent her. I was fixated on it.

I almost didn't send it. I almost acted like a coward and let her leave me.

If Daniel hadn't convinced me to get my sorry ass out of the bar, I might not be here now.

You need to stop pushing me away, I texted her. I don't know what the hell your problem is, but you've got to stop this shit. I'm coming over.

She didn't reply. I didn't expect her to, but I was still coming to get her.

I was thinking about what I was going to say and how I was going to say it. It felt like it was my last chance. The Hail Mary of getting her back but also keeping her. And then I heard her.

My boots slapped on her porch as I picked up my pace.

My fists slammed on the door as I called out her name.

But I could barely hear them over the sound of the chaotic pounding in my chest, the sound of my blood rushing in my ears.

The sound of her screaming out again. With fear.

My shoulder crashed into the door without thinking twice. The pain rippled up my neck and down my back.

"Allie!" I screamed her name as the wood cracked and I

shoved myself into the room. She was right there but still so far away.

The sight will be burned into my memory forever.

The scratch on Kevin's arm, deep and bright in color, the redness in Allie's skin and clear fear written on her face, cheeks tearstained and her voice raw and hoarse as she screamed again. How he was hovering over her, shoving her down even as he looked up at me.

Red.

It's all red.

I don't know how my body moved, but it did. I don't think I breathed until I picked up the lamp.

I remember him getting up and I could see him thinking about how to play it off. I could see the look in his eyes. Like he wasn't actually hurting her. Like I'd just caught him playing around.

The lamp was so light in my grasp. As though it weighed nothing as I whacked him over the head with it. My body was tight and screaming. It took no energy at all. No thought. His head was the part of him closest to me as he stood. The easiest to strike.

The sound is something I don't think I'll ever forget either. The crack of the lamp, the crunch of his bones.

The blow was solid. Even though his wrist blocked the first swing, the next bash of the lamp struck him right where I aimed. The cord swung around, whipping him in the face and then back to my arm. I aimed again as he yelled at me to stop.

And I know I aimed. I can remember that.

Again and again, my arm lifted and slammed the lamp down. My throat burned with a scream I couldn't hear. I pushed my muscles harder and harder, feeling like I was on fire.

I just wanted her to stop screaming. I wanted all this to go away. To be a nightmare and nothing more.

For a moment, I questioned myself. As if my sudden lapse of sanity was over. As if I wasn't angry, and I was wondering what I was doing.

But the moment was quickly forgotten when I heard Allie scream again.

And that's when the hammering of the base of the lamp turned to a slash from the broken ceramic.

It's all a haze of red.

Like I wasn't seeing things clearly. Like it wasn't real.

It stayed that way as the blood spilled from his neck where a shard of the glass pierced his skin. It covered his shoulder and poured onto my leg and onto the sofa. I've never seen anything like it. And maybe the surprise of it is what stops me. I can't be sure.

His eyes stare through me. With every breath, I wait for him to blink but he doesn't. What the hell just happened? My heart pounds and my pulse is louder than anything I've ever heard. I'm dizzy as I imagine him reaching up to stop the steady flow of blood, but his body is still. *This isn't real. This didn't happen.*

I can barely hear Allie but I know her screams have stopped, and she's saying something else now as she hunches over, but not taking her eyes from me. Something laced with dread and guilt, but I can't hear her over the ringing in my ears. I can hardly focus my vision on her. My body's shaking and I can't move. I'm frozen. It feels that way as I drop what's left of the lamp to the floor. It thuds and then cracks, that's clear to me. But Allie's words are mixed with the memory of her scream.

I can hardly feel her tugging on me as I stare at her ripped pajamas, hanging from her chest.

It all stays red until the scream from behind me forces me to realize there's someone else here. Someone other than Allie. Allie's weeping on the ground, her hands covered in blood as she crouches on the ground and then looks up at me with fear and sorrow swirling in her eyes and it takes another scream before I turn around to face the front door and see who's screaming.

Someone who would bear witness to what I'd done.

Someone who heard the screaming and came in through the front door.

Someone who saw Kevin's dead body at my feet.

Allie's neighbor from earlier, is screaming in the doorway behind me.

Chapter 31

Allison

No. I take it back.

I take it all back.

This wasn't supposed to happen.

"Dean, stop!" I try to scream at him but my voice is hoarse, the pain ripping my throat as I topple over. The bleeding won't stop. I keep pushing against Kevin's throat with my trembling hands as if I can stop the flow. But it won't.

It's too late.

I know it is but I can't stop trying.

I can barely breathe as my shaking hands move away from the limp body. He's still warm but blood isn't pumping from the wound anymore. It's hardly a trickle.

"Are you okay?" I hear Dean ask over the sound of a shrill scream.

It takes me a moment to realize he's trying to pick me up and move me, but I can't move. I can't be touched. I only catch a glimpse of a woman's back from the doorway.

My heart races and my body chills.

"Dean," I say. *What did I do?*

It happened so fast. Too fast to control. Too many moving parts to see what would come next.

I didn't mean for this to happen. I try to blink away the vision. The memory. As the feeling of Kevin pushing me down comes back to me and I could vomit from it. I shove against Dean's chest. My body reacts reflexively, trying to protect me.

"It's me," he says as I wrap my arms around my shoulders and try to get away.

I'm numb and shaking.

"It's me. It's okay. It's okay." Dean keeps speaking lies.

It's not okay.

It's never been worse.

Kevin's body is at an odd angle on the floor and as I try to back away, Dean's boot hits Kevin's leg. And it moves easily, lifeless.

I didn't mean for him to die.

It's all I can think. I swear. I wanted the world to know who he was and what he was capable of.

I wanted him to pay for what he did to Sam.

But I never intended this.

"I'm sorry," I say, the words whispered from my lips and Dean stiffens beside me. It's the first time I really look up at him.

His hair's disheveled and his eyes are narrowed and deadly. I should be scared of him, but all I can do is cling to his side.

"You didn't do anything." His t-shirt seems to tighten around his broad shoulders, the cotton stretching as he takes a heavy breath.

But didn't I? The pain and regret all mix with everything else. It's a whirlwind of chaos.

Right there beside us is the undeniable and crushing truth that I've brought Dean into this. I led him here. The one person who made me question it.

My heart stutters in my chest, refusing to believe this is real and not wanting to admit any of this. I just want to go back to that night in the hotel room and tell him everything. I want to beg for his forgiveness. To let him walk away and save him.

It's too late.

The whisper hangs between us as I say, "What have I done?"

"You were fighting him," Dean says and struggles to control his breathing. I can feel his eyes piercing into me but I can't look him in the eyes. "You were fighting him and screaming," he repeats.

I nod my head.

"He was hurting you." His voice cracks on the last word.

I finally look up at him with tears welling in my eyes.

The pain has apparently won. Of all things, pain is the most damaging. "He was trying to…" The words are slow, achingly slow and the worst word of all stays trapped in the back of my throat.

I'm going to be sick.

My stomach churns and I try to stand but my head's foggy and I slip backward, almost touching the dead body.

With the image of him pushing me down, I try to get away and Dean's there, holding me, pulling me away from the nonexistent threat. *This wasn't supposed to happen.*

"I'm here," he whispers and holds me as the faint sound of a siren in the distance sneaks in through the broken front door. "It's okay."

"Dean, it's not okay." I look into his eyes as I speak and I'm so wounded. None of this is okay. It hasn't been. But it wasn't supposed to become this. This isn't right.

What have I done? Please, I just want to take it back.

My heart pounds in my chest. The fear is crippling.

"No." The word bubbles from my lips repeatedly as the reality hits me. There's no way I could have known this is what would happen. I didn't know. I swear I didn't know and I didn't want this.

"It's okay. You're okay," Dean keeps saying even over the sound of the sirens growing louder by the minute. As if anything could be okay.

"You don't understand," I plead with him to listen but my

throat is scratchy, and I hiccup over my words. "I'm so sorry," I whimper, covering my face as the tears pour from me.

"Stop saying you're sorry!" Dean yells as he grips my shoulders, forcing me to face him. His strong hands pin me where he wants me with a force that almost makes me collapse. If I did, I'd collapse into his arms. "You didn't do anything wrong," he says and his voice is full of sympathy, but so much more than that too. He keeps saying that but he doesn't know the truth.

"You don't understand," I say, the words full of agony as I remember Samantha's broad smile. She was so beautiful. So full of life and happiness. It's a smile that will only live in my memory. I've let everyone down. Everyone I ever loved. Sam. *Dean.*

"Did you want him to do that?" Dean questions with hate, with denial, with jealousy in his eyes and I shake my head furiously.

"Never," I tell him quickly. "I didn't. I swear."

"Then stop it!" he commands me. He doesn't understand.

"I knew he would," I say, the words coming out strained. "When I let him in—" It's only a part of a confession and it's cut off by Dean's fingers digging into my arms as he shakes me slightly.

My cheeks feel hot as the tears stain them.

"He's responsible for what he did, Allie," Dean tells me, his eyes piercing into my own. "I won't have you say any differently." The sirens are louder now, almost deafening.

"I asked for this," I say weakly, full of shame.

"What did you ask for?" He barely gets out the words as his voice shakes with pain. He shakes his head as he adds, "You didn't ask for this." He's full of denial as the police park in front of the house. I can hear them. There's more than one cop car and the sound of multiple doors slamming shut is mixed with him whispering that this isn't my fault and that I'm okay and that he's the one who's sorry.

But it is my fault.

I asked for this. For vengeance. For justice.

I didn't just ask for it. I prayed for it every day for years. When they taunted her in the hallways. When the other girls declined to sit with her. Every meeting I had with lawyers who refused to take the case, saying it was impossible. Every time I thought of her, I knew I would never be able to stop until someone did something. I prayed for him to pay.

Dean didn't, though. Knowing that, I hate myself even more.

Chapter 32

Dean

My stomach feels hollow.

My body is freezing.

The fucking jail cell is cold, so at least that part makes sense. The doctor who came in to examine me said I was in shock. Maybe that's what happens when you kill a man. Or when you see someone you love screaming in pain. Maybe the two are the same.

A cell opens and closes, and I barely lift my eyes at the eerie sound of finality.

I killed him.

In cold blood.

This isn't a bar fight I can get out of.

Charges have been pressed and they booked me within hours.

Third-degree murder.

I told them everything. Every bit of what I remembered. There's no way to get out of this and I still don't know how I could do it. I can say I'm sorry and I didn't intend to kill him, and I mean it. I do. I didn't mean to kill the prick. It doesn't change it, though. I can't take it back.

I'm fucked.

I run my hand down my face and try to stop seeing him. Any time the image flashes in my head of him dead on the floor, it's followed by one of him on top of Allie. It's like a sick joke my mind's playing on me. Twisting and coiling the darkness inside my head until it strikes me down over and over again.

"Allie," I whisper under my breath and let my head fall. The door opens at the end of the row of cells and I repeat to myself, "It was to protect her." Wasn't it?

I'm already starting to question it. Just like the cops did. Asking me what I thought of him. If we'd had physical encounters before. How my anger management sessions were going. Whether I tried to pull him away or if I just went in to kill him.

They questioned if he was even hurting her.

I didn't have to keep going, but I swear I couldn't stop myself.

There were so many questions, I couldn't even keep my own answers straight.

"Just let me know when you're ready to leave." I lift my eyes at the sound of the guard's voice and see Uncle Rob standing outside of the bars.

They slide open and he walks through, looking like a ghost of the man I once knew. His hair's silver and the heavy bags under his eyes are either from years of booze or weeks of no sleep.

"Dean," he says my name and my eyes drop from his jeans to his boots, then lower to the cement floor of the cell. I can't look him in the eyes.

The cell door shuts with a loud clink and I hear him walk over to the cold bench to sit beside me.

He doesn't speak as he leans forward with his elbows on his knees.

"Your lawyer's coming," he tells me with a tone of comfort and safety as though a lawyer can get me out of this. I guess I should have asked for one before saying a word. But what's the point?

"I did it," I tell him in a tight voice and tilt my head to reach his eyes. "I killed him." The last sentence comes out strong. I can at least own it. "He was trying to—"

Uncle Rob cuts me off, placing a hand on my shoulder and leaning in closer. "I know what happened. They gave me the report. But that doesn't mean you don't need a lawyer."

His eyes are bloodshot and rimmed in red as he stares at me, begging me to hear him out.

"I don't see the point. I told them what happened. They

know he tried to rape her." My voice goes tight. "I only did it to save her."

"It's Jack's nephew. He's friends with the judge. You need a lawyer." His voice is hard but also panicked.

I huff out a breath of disbelief at my uncle's words. "I already know that."

"Listen to me for once in your fucking life, Dean," my uncle shouts at me with exasperation. "He doesn't want his name smeared."

"Smeared?" I can't believe what I'm hearing.

"You don't know how they'll spin it," my uncle says sharply and that gets my attention.

"Spin it?"

"Jack said she set his nephew up."

"She what?" My vision spins.

"That she liked it that way and wanted to make you jealous."

"You believe him?" I stand up abruptly, moving away from my uncle and looking at him with disgust.

"No!" he says and taps his foot nervously on the cement floor. "They're going to try to spin it. They're saying she wanted him and that you caught them in the act."

"But she's a witness, she can testify. Shit, a neighbor heard her screaming!" My voice bellows in the cell, my anger bouncing off the hard, unforgiving walls.

"Well, there's some damning evidence, Dean. You need to

hear it. You need to be prepared for it."

"Hear what?"

"Your anger, your arrests. Pictures of the two of you and testimonies of her being *more than friendly* with some of your friends." My heart slows with each word.

"None of that has anything to do with this."

"Maybe not to you, but your opinion doesn't matter. If they think she's lying, her testimony doesn't matter."

"It's the truth!"

"It doesn't matter," he says in a flat voice.

"She didn't want him to rape her."

"You have to prove it was rape."

"Her word isn't enough?" I spit back at him with even more contempt.

"Not when she's made her intentions questionable. The DA has to decide—"

"Get out!" I say and seethe. "I don't need you or your lawyer." My voice comes out even and confident, and I have no fucking clue how. I'm trembling with anger and sickness.

"I'm not leaving you," he tells me with a shaky voice. "You needed me back then, and I failed you. I won't fail you now. If you don't want me here, that's fine. I'll respect that, but I'm getting you a lawyer for the arraignment."

Chapter 33

Allison

I've been waiting for one phone call.

The one where a stranger on the end of the line will tell me I can go see him. They told me I needed to leave. That I needed to wait and stop calling. So, I'm trying to be patient.

I have to tell Dean first. He has to know.

And then I can tell everyone else. They'll let Dean go after I do. They'll have to.

It's my fault. I'm still in disbelief. I can't believe it happened.

My tired eyes lift from the dead violets on the windowsill to the front door. The window's open and I should have heard someone pull up to the house, but I didn't.

"Allison?" a soft voice says hesitantly and I press my palms into my sore eyes.

"Mom?" Through my tears, I think I see her. She's hazy and the white blinds swirl in front of her before she can walk in and shut the door behind her, but I hear her voice.

"You didn't answer your phone." She talks quickly as she walks toward me with uncertain steps. "I had to come see you," she whispers as I get up from the floor with shaky legs.

"Mom?" I can't stop repeating myself.

My feet move on their own, guiding me to her and when I finally get close enough, I cling to her. Burying my face in the crook of her neck, I hold on to her with a tight grip.

"Mom," I say between the sobs.

"I'm here," she says and holds me back just as tightly, the keys in her hand dropping to the floor and clattering together. The noise makes my shoulders shake, but everything makes me jumpy now. I don't care.

I've broken down so many times in the last week. I thought I was done with crying. I thought I had nothing left, but as she cries into my hair and rocks me, they come again. They're merciless.

I deserve it.

"Are you okay?" my mother asks me although her grip doesn't loosen. I can't nod and I can't speak, so I don't say anything until she holds me at arm's length.

"Talk to me please," she begs me and I shake my head. Her eyes are red and puffy with dark shadows beneath them.

"I'm not okay. I'm not okay," I tell her as my shoulders shake.

"It's okay, I'm here," she says, just like Dean did. As if mere words can make it all right but they can't. "I heard what happened," my mother says and my body tenses, but all she says is that it will be okay.

"It's all my fault." The words pour from me even though I'm not sure they make sense. I'm not sure she can even comprehend them.

"Shhh." Hushed words won't keep me quiet. Not anymore.

"You don't understand," I say and the words come out quickly, the rest begging to follow. To confess.

"I do understand. I know that boy's name. I know who he is," she says and her gaze turns hard and full of worry. "You can't tell them you knew. They won't look into it. Don't tell them you knew." Her throat's tight as she swallows and it takes a moment for the realization to hit me with full force. She knows. Maybe not all of it, but she knows.

"I have to—"

"It's not your fault," she says, cutting me off. "What happened to Sam wasn't your fault either and—"

"Yes, it was!" I scream at the audacity of my mother saying such a lie. Especially now. How dare she! I shove against her, knocking myself backward and scramble to leave her comfort. "When will you admit it?" I shout at her, letting the pain and anger twist in my gut. "I knew the truth and I didn't fight for her! I didn't help her!" I practically hiss, the shame and regret all-consuming as I say, "I walked away because you told me to."

My mother shakes her head, denying it as she always has. Her hands are up in defense as if she's approaching a wounded animal ready to run. Her blonde hair brushes back and forth around her shoulders. "It wasn't your fault," she tries to say again but her words are lost as she cries into her hand. "None of this is your fault and I'll protect you, baby. They won't find out."

"If I hadn't texted her," I say then gulp in air and my body shudders. "If I hadn't told her you didn't want me to see her anymore ..." I close my eyes, remembering how I sent the text in anger. I was so upset that my mother would treat Sam the same way everyone else did. Like it was her fault that Kevin had hurt her. Like she was lying about what he'd done to her.

My mother blamed Sam. And I spread that blame to my friend. My friend who was struggling. Who just needed someone to love her. I broke Sam by telling her that. I know I did. I didn't agree with my mother. I wasn't going to leave her. But I wasn't given the chance to show her. I sent that message without thinking what it would do.

My mother was just like them. She said Sam was trouble, and I should never have turned my back on Sam. I should never have acted so rashly.

That was the last text I sent to Sam. And the last one she read before she killed herself.

"Admit it," I demand with a note of finality in my voice. "Admit it, Mother!"

"It's not—" she starts to say but I cut her off, refusing to listen to her denial after all this time. Her shoulders shake with a sob she tries to silence.

"Why avoid me then? Why walk around like you're guilty? So quiet and afraid to say anything to me like your words will break me? Why!" I scream at her. I was quiet for too long. All of this waiting to come out and instead it only festered inside.

Both of us were so aware of how our words had killed, that neither of us spoke. I hate her for it. So quiet, I became dead inside. She's the one I blame because I'd rather blame her than myself.

"For years, you hardly spoke to me. You let me get away with anything and everything. You avoided me. You know how much you meant to her. You knew how it would hurt her. And you didn't care! You didn't care about her and now she's dead!"

My voice is hoarse and the words echo in my head. I didn't care about Sam when I sent that to her. I was just angry at my mom for not believing me. I didn't think about how it would destroy Sam. It was my fault for telling her. It's always been my fault.

"I'm sorry!" my mother wails. "I wish I could take it back, Allison, but I can't and I'm sorry." Her face is bright red, and she struggles to swallow as she waits for my response. "I'm so sorry. I didn't want to hurt her. I never wanted to hurt her. I just wanted to save you."

It's the first time she's ever told me she regrets it. It's so late. Too late for what really matters but still, it's something I desperately want to cling to.

How could I ever be saved in a world that allowed this to happen? In a world that makes a victim feel like they could have stopped it when there wasn't a damn thing they could have done to prevent the inevitable. There's nothing that can save me.

"Please stop hating me," she begs, her bottom lip wobbling and her frail shoulders shaking. I always thought she was so strong. I thought I was the weak one. Maybe we're both weak.

"I never hated you," I tell her but I can't be sure that it's honest. Pain turns to hate so easily. "I wasn't okay, though. It's not okay. It never will be."

"Please forgive me."

I nod my head although I flinch when she tries to hug me, and it breaks her. I can't help it. There's so much more. And the truth begs me to speak it.

My voice is eerily calm and my mother just nods her head once, staring at the pot of withered violets and avoiding my gaze. Or maybe my judgment.

"Mom, I have to tell you something."

My mother's eyes whip to mine. Maybe because the tone of my voice has changed. From pained to haunted.

"When Grandmom died, that very week, there was an article."

My mom wipes her face with the sleeve of her shirt, but I know she's listening.

"There was a name I recognized." My hands clench at my side as I remember seeing it. "The name of the boy who hurt Sam." The words hurt as they leave me and the article flashes in my memory.

"You don't need to tell me this." There's hesitation in her voice like she's scared to know.

I hear her and I know she already assumes, but she should know. I want the world to know what I did. "Just about alumni, about tradition. It wasn't anything that should have made me angry, but it did. I was the angriest I've ever been." I admit to her something I've never said out loud. Jack and Kevin Henderson, the proud alumni nephew. Smiling in an article.

The boy whose uncle was friends with a judge.

The boy who said she'd made him think it was what she wanted.

The boy who went back home and kissed other girls and smiled, knowing he'd get what he wanted. *No matter what.*

That boy never paid for what he did. He smiled at me. "Sam could never smile again, but there he was, smiling."

"Allison?" she says, and my mother's tone holds a warning. Like she knows what's coming. Like she's followed my train of thought.

"I'm not done," I tell her and her expression changes. I force my clammy hands to unclench.

"I came here because of that article. I came here because I wanted him to do to me, what he did to Sam."

"No," she says and shakes her head, denying it, the puzzle pieces firmly falling into place for her. *I asked for it.* Her head shakes as I continue my story. She can say those words now like she did back then. It'll be true this time.

"I wanted the world to see him for the person he was. I wanted them to know she wasn't lying." My words get louder as I speak. More frantic, more saddened. "She deserved some kind of justice. I came here and I sought him out on purpose."

Her cries are all that stop me from telling her more. She covers her mouth with both hands and shakes her head.

I won't deny it. I won't pretend things aren't as they seem.

"I knew what I was doing, Mom. I wanted him to hurt me. Because if he did it to me, he'd be punished. Sam would finally have some sort of justice. It wouldn't make it right, but she'd have something." I croak out the last word, the tears slipping down my face to my chin and falling hard on the floor beneath me. Each one feeling heavier than the last.

I walked away six years ago, perfectly fine on the outside. Nothing happened to me. I was saved by circumstance. But what happened to Sam, not only that night but the weeks after, forever changed whatever it is that makes a person a person.

Death changes people.

So does hate.

That's all I've been since Sam died. Hateful.

I know my hate came from fear, it came from regret. It was bred from sadness.

In six years, all I've been doing is suffering. *Until I met Dean.* It hurts. Whatever heaviness was lifted from my shoulders by my confession comes crashing back down tenfold.

"You can't tell anyone, Allison," my mother speaks with tears brimming in her eyes. She cups her hands around the sides of my face like a mother does and pleads with me. "They can't know. Don't tell them. Don't give them a reason to blame you."

"But Dean," I start, and my voice is tight. The second I say his name, my phone rings.

Chapter 34

Dean

Exhausted isn't even close to the right word. Terrified doesn't do it justice either. Both are nothing compared to the concoction that flows through my veins as I sit here. Still, I don't feel either. All I feel is the pain for my Allie Cat, sitting on the other side of the plexiglass wall.

"You only have ten minutes," the guard reminds me before stalking off. I don't turn to look at him. Instead I take in Allison, the darkness under her eyes and the dress that hangs delicately on her slender frame. Her hair's brushed back and falls around her shoulders. She tried to look good for me. Although her mascara doesn't stay in place when she wipes under her eyes before desperately reaching for the phone.

One on her side, one on mine. There are eight other stations like this. Only two others are being used, though.

I don't make her wait long before picking up the phone and breathing her name.

"Are you okay?" she asks but her voice is strained, and then she lowers her gaze, closing her eyes tight. *Don't look away. Please.*

My hand against the glass brings her attention back to me and she's quick to put her hand on the other side. As if magically the barrier between us would vanish at her touch.

She swallows thickly and tells me, "I know you're not. I'm so sorry, Dean. I—"

"I'm all right," I say, cutting her off and remind her, "I've done this before, you know."

"It isn't the same."

"I know."

"I'm so sorry," she cries even though I shush her. She keeps saying it as she unravels in front of me.

Even on the phone, the sound of her swallowing thickly is audible. "Dean, I have to tell you something," she says and her voice begs for mercy she doesn't think she deserves.

"Is it about the case?"

"Yes and—"

"Don't say a word."

"I have to—"

"No." My voice is sharp and her eyes strike me with both

surprise and pain. As if the single word was venomous too.

"You won't say anything here. Where there are other people who can hear you. record you."

"Dean, you don't understand," she says then pulls her hand away from mine as she shakes her head, but I keep mine in place.

"I do. I understand more than you realize, Allie Cat." My expression softens and when it does, hers mirrors mine, softening with a sadness. Her bottom lip trembles when I say her nickname and my throat goes tight as I swallow down the pain of it all.

"Give me something I can dream about in here and I'll make whatever it is come true when I'm out," I tell her and even though it's spoken like a command, I'm desperate for it.

The tips of my fingers slip on the glass and they get her attention. She's quick to put her hand back and her head drops down, her eyes never leaving mine, though.

"Don't let me see you sad, Allie," I say, consoling her in a whisper over the phone. "I need something to dream about."

Removing her hand for only a moment to wipe under her eyes, she sniffles and then tells me, "I miss you in bed at night."

"Oh yeah?" I comment with an asymmetric smile and she heaves in air, attempting to keep herself from crying although it doesn't work.

My heart breaks a million times for her and it'll break a million more with every tear she sheds.

"I miss you too. At night and always. I miss your sassy

mouth and stupid jokes."

She huffs a laugh and wipes her tears again. "Mine aren't stupid, yours are stupid." Her rebuttal makes both of us smile.

"You should get a big pillow. Like one of those long ones while I'm gone."

"Dean." She says my name like it pains her, closing her eyes tight.

"Look at me, Allie Cat." She responds to my command without hesitation, waiting with her lips parted and her body at the ready.

"Get a long pillow, and hold it at night." I force a grin when I tell her, "It's the only thing allowed in your bed until I get out of here. You hear me?"

She barely laughs and the sound is saddened, but she does and presses her hand against the glass again, its warmth coming through to me.

"It's only you, Dean," she confesses, her voice lowered and full of sincerity on the line. "You're the only man I want and love."

The itch at the back of my throat and the prick at the back of my eyes is hard to hide, but I do it for her. "About time you told me," I respond and a genuine smile paired with a huff of a laugh from my Allie Cat is my reward. "I love you too, Allison."

She's got to know I love her. And that makes this worth it. I would do anything for her.

Chapter 35

Allison

"We just have a few more questions." There are two detectives in the room and I can tell the men apart from their voices and picture exactly how their lips move with each word without looking up from the pile of chipped nail polish I picked off in the last hour I've been sitting here.

"Explain the altercation again," the other cop, Detective Massing asks and then the other, Detective Ballinger, adds, "At what point, exactly, did your ex decide to pick up the lamp?"

My mother begged me not to come in at all. She said I legally could decline. She's afraid I'm going to say something I shouldn't. Truth be told, right now I'm afraid too. I made a promise to her though, that I wouldn't tell them. That's because I'm going to tell them all the truth when I'm on the stand. I have to. My eyes prick with tears. It's the only way to save Dean. I have to save him. That's the only reason I've been sitting in this chair.

"I told you, he didn't decide." My voice cracks and my eyes gloss over remembering the haunted look on his face. "I was screaming before the door burst open and when I looked up, he saw what was happening. He ripped him off of me without thinking at all." I watch it all unfold again, barely breathing. I see it every night, a memory that will stay with me forever.

"And then?"

"And then he picked up the lamp and I yelled for him to stop from where I was, but he was so fast and ..." I trail off and my eyes lift to meet theirs as I continue, "it was over before I could even breathe."

"And then what did he do? Did he attempt to conceal the weapon?"

"He didn't even seem to know what he'd done. Dean approached me and tried to reach out for me and there was so much blood on his arms."

"From bludgeoning his friend to death," the asshole one says. Ballinger. I ignore him and my response is only a whisper when I say, "It was like he didn't realize."

"How is it Dean entered your place of residence?"

I blink at him. "He opened the door.

"So you didn't have it locked?"

"I ..." I have to think back to whether I did or not and Kevin's eyes stare back at me.

Do you want to come in? Was that what I asked him? My bottom lip quivers with the visions playing in front of me.

"I asked if you had it locked," Ballinger repeats with a hardened tone. As if reliving the moment just before trauma and tragedy doesn't take more than a second to get through.

Swallowing thickly, I answer him, I didn't even close the door. The vision of Kevin kicking it shut as I tried to sway, deliberately appearing drunk takes over.

"So he didn't need a key to get in."

"No, anyone could have opened that door to help me."

They don't like it when I say *help me*. They quiet down and share a glance each time I say it. But that's what Dean was doing. He came in to rescue me because I was screaming and in return, I made him a murderer. I don't know how he'll ever forgive me. But so long as he doesn't pay for my sins, I'll be able to sleep at night. At least I pray I will.

"You said you were screaming," Massing starts then takes a long inhale. The air conditioner kicks on in the quiet room with a click. It's empty except for us, another uncomfortable as fuck chair next to me, and a folder containing Dean's rap sheet sitting in the middle of the table. "And that's because Kevin was on top of you?"

"Yes, he was forcing my clothes off."

"And did you at any time, help him?" Ballinger asks and I peer up at both of them, unflinchingly looking back at me.

"Help him?"

"To remove your clothes," he clarifies. I've never felt so disgusted and the emotions that swell up inside of me are a mix of raw pain and fear and anger. It's all of it, all at once.

"I want a lawyer." My statement is simple and I damn well mean it. My throat is sore and the words raspy, but clear.

"You don't need one; you haven't been charged with anything."

"So I'm free to go then?" My voice is flat, my lips pressed in a thin line.

"We have more questions."

"I won't be answering any without a lawyer." For the first time since I walked in here, I speak with authority.

"Why is that?" Massing asks.

"Do you have something to hide?" Ballinger says with a sneer.

My entire body is tight with a pain neither of these two pricks will ever know.

"You aren't just questioning me. You're questioning what I already told you ... maybe that's your job, but mine is to get a lawyer."

Chapter 36

Dean

So many eyes are on me as I sit here in the hard wooden chair. There's only one gaze that calls to me, though. One that begs me to look back.

Allison.

She's so close, yet unreachable. All I can hear as my lawyer and the district attorney go back and forth in front of the judge is my heart racing, begging me to turn to her and ease the worry and pain I know she's feeling.

She's staring at me like that day in class when I first got the balls to talk to her. That day she gave into me. I can feel her staring at me like I did her, but I can't resist her the way she did with me. I never could.

When I turn to face her, I can't stand the look in her eyes. It's clear she blames herself. I would give anything to go to her, but I have to rip my gaze away.

I don't know where we stand. If she hates me. Condemns me. Loves me. *Please God, let her love me still.* I'd do anything for her.

My throat's tight, as is the pain in my chest when my lawyer argues in my defense. It's only an arraignment and my lawyer said the case they have is weak.

A plea of not guilty by reason of temporary insanity is my best bet for surviving this and I don't object to it.

Judge Hubert is an old man. The years are shown through the wrinkles around his pale blue eyes and the white beard around his scowl.

His gaze lingers on me while the prosecutor reads the statement from the psychologist who examined my initial confession.

It's more evidence but at least the shrink supports my case. Not that the prosecutor sees it that way. He's doing his damnedest to make sure this goes to trial. A plea of temporary insanity isn't applicable, according to him. Every time his hard voice booms in the courtroom, my hands clench into fists. If he were in my position, I can't imagine he'd do any different.

I just want to get out of here. In my head, I imagine them letting me walk out right now so I can go straight to Allie. So I can finally talk to her.

I don't know if she's all right. I know she refused medical help. I know he didn't get a chance to ... I have to clear the lump in my throat at the thought, a chill rolling down my spine and making me that much more tense. I overheard some cops talking about it. For that reason alone, all of this is worth it. Even if it weakens my case.

At least I saved her from that.

Still, I need to hear her say she's okay. I need to hear it from her.

I'm only able to take a quick glance, just one. As soon as our eyes lock, hers well up with a sadness I hate. With a pain I wish I could take from her. And she apologizes. *Again.*

"Your honor, our case is strong. There was nothing my client could have done given his mental state when he arrived on the scene." My lawyer, Nina Abbot, speaks clearly and confidently. As if there's no greater truth than the words she's made echo throughout the courtroom. "He was unaware of reality. In that moment, he was not aware of what he was doing. Only his motions, not what they would result in."

I force my gaze back to the wooden table in front of me. It's smooth and smells like lemon as if it was just polished before we came out here.

It's difficult to breathe as she places her hand on my shoulder. "It's obvious given my client's testimony and the report just read from Dr. Agostino that given the situation, Mr. Warren was not in his right mind to control his actions."

"That only holds true if in fact the testimony from both Mr. Warren and Allison Parker are reliable, and there are questions surrounding the validity of Miss Parker's statement." The prosecutor's voice rings out and my fists turn white knuckled. I keep my gaze down, refusing to look at him and his tailored suit. The image of his face is clear in my mind as I keep my shoulders and neck stiff. His jaw is hard and cleanly shaven. His eyes cold and unforgiving. He's a man who will fight to put me behind bars at all cost. The very thought should be terrifying as I sit here, because I did it. I murdered him. But I did it for her. *And I'd do it again.*

"With all due respect, Miss Parker's statement is irrelevant. Mr. Warren's mental state was determined by his perception when he arrived on the property. The same perception that the third witness, Mrs. Clemons, the adjacent neighbor who witnessed the end of the act, gave. As far as my client and Mrs. Clemons could both tell, Miss Parker was in imminent danger. Whether or not she's even capable or willing to testify is irrelevant."

The sound of the courtroom doors opening beg me to look behind me, but I resist. My body's tight and my muscles coiled. I hardly trust myself to breathe. I can still feel Allie looking at me. I refuse to move unless it's to go to her.

It's only when my lawyer turns away from me and the soft whispers of furious voices make the rest of the room turn silent, that I force myself to look in my periphery.

The sound of two people walking down the aisle draws my attention more. A skinny young woman, dressed in black slacks and a loose, cream blouse, is hidden by the silhouette of the man beside her but as they walk, her face comes into view.

I think her name is Angie. She has the same chem lecture as Allison and me and I've seen her around a few times. She stands just past Mr. Beck, the prosecutor, and next to another man in a suit. I turn my head to make sure it's her. Her blonde curls dangle in front of her face and I'm sure she's doing it on purpose.

She's ashamed. Even as she stands there, clasping her hands in front of her, she starts to cry. Silent tears that she quickly wipes away.

"Your honor, new evidence has just come to our attention and we'd like a recess." Mr. Beck finally addresses the court, although his voice is laced with something that gives me hope.

Defeat.

"What is this new evidence?" the judge asks, his pale blue eyes moving between Angie and the man who brought her in.

"The prosecution's defense rests heavily on the questionability of Miss Parker's statement that Mr. Henderson was forcing himself on her. A witness has come forward stating the action of Mr. Henderson is a repeated offense."

"As in, he attempted to rape her?" the judge clarifies and Angie lowers her head, tears falling freely, and this time she doesn't brush them away.

"Charges were pressed in early August, but the case

was never brought to court. The charges were dismissed." The quiet air of the room changes, turning to whispers and murmurs. Back in early August I hadn't been accepted into the program yet. But Kevin was here then at his parents' place.

"Your honor," Mr. Beck says, "the case was never—"

"They settled out of court?" the judge asks, cutting off Mr. Beck and the district attorney shakes his head no.

"The witness refused to testify and dropped the charges."

The judge taps his pointer finger on the gavel in front of him, considering her and the new information.

"I'm sorry," I hear Angie say in a tight voice. She's trying to whisper but it's useless in a room where everyone's watching her. Her shoulders are hunched and trembling as she pleads with Allie to understand, "I should have told you sooner. I was so ashamed. I didn't want anyone to know."

Chapter 37

Allison

The air is cold for only being October. It doesn't help that it's late, dark, and I'm standing in the shadow outside of the jail.

Even with the chill in my bones and the wind whipping around my face, I'm hot. It's from the anxiety.

I don't even think I can feel anything really. At least, I wasn't until the double glass doors open and Dean walks out of them.

My eyes don't stray from the entrance as he strides forward, looking to his left and right. I don't recognize the clothes he's in; they must be new or maybe the lawyer brought them to him so he had clothes to leave in. Dark jeans and a crisp white polo look odd on him as he passes under the streetlight just outside of the doors, but he's never looked better to me. I've never wanted him more.

He's free. Free to go with no charges pressed. There isn't enough evidence to support a trial for what they charged him with.

I want to take him away before anyone can say anything differently.

All I have in me is a shaky half step forward, but I can't move any farther. He may be free from all of this but I'm not, and I don't deserve to be. The sheer terror of what this confession will do to me is enough to keep me cemented in place.

It's enough that he sees me. The small motion makes him look at me and when he does, everything changes.

"Allie." The way he says my name frees me from the spot I've been chained to. I run to him as quickly as my body will allow. Crashing my chest against his and holding him with a fierceness I've never felt before. As if letting go of him would mean losing him. I can't lose him. *Please God, let him love me still.*

"Are you okay?" we both say at nearly the same time. His hands travel from my cheeks to my arms, then lower. As if checking every part of me and making sure I'm all right. Apart from a few bruises, there's nothing on the outside that's hurt.

I can barely nod as I look him over. He spent days in jail and was charged with murder. All because of me.

"Everything's okay. It's over. It's okay." He repeats himself as he kisses my hair. As if it really is but I know all too well that it's not. With a heavy inhale I get a whiff of his scent and

I hold onto him tighter, refusing to let go. I have to tell him. He deserves to know it's my fault. He wanted the truth and I owe him that much.

"Dean." When I say his name, my voice cracks and his eyes spark with slight fear. The same fear that runs through my own blood.

"Let's get out of here," is his only response as his dark eyes pierce into mine. "Let's just go."

"Where are you going?" I ask him as my heart pounds and I barely get out the words. The dreaded sickness stirs in my belly. I have to tell him. That's why I refuse to let his hand go. It may be the last time I ever hold him.

The sound of a passing car in the street behind us catches my attention, but I feel Dean's gaze and it never leaves me.

"I don't care. Anywhere," he says while still staring deep into my eyes.

"It sounds a lot like running away to me," I tell him honestly with a shaky breath. The bitter wind of the cold night whips by us and it only makes each of us move closer to the other. I'm on the edge of falling again but this time, I don't want to stop myself. I almost don't want to tell him. I want to run away with him. So long as I'm with him.

"Maybe sometimes," he says then pauses and takes my hand in his, taking a step closer to me. I have to lift my head to look him in the eyes. "Maybe sometimes it's okay to run away."

"I thought we were only supposed to run toward

something?" I remind him.

"I don't give a fuck what you call it, Allie. As long as I'm running with you, that's all that matters to me."

My eyes close and I lean into Dean's hard chest. His strong arms wrap around me and I cling to him. "Can we forget the past?" I ask him softly, my question lingering in the heat between us. "I don't want to remember any of it anymore."

I can feel the urge to lie. To keep it all a secret. My heart begs me not to speak the truth. It wants Dean too much.

"Whatever you want to forget, I'll help you," he whispers and his voice sounds pained. He still loves me. The pitter-patter in my chest hurts.

My fingers skim along his shirt and my conscience begs me to confess to him, at war with everything else. The moment my lips part, his finger slips down against my lips.

I shake my head away from his fingers, refusing his protest to not say it. It's now or never, and I can't let it be never.

"Dean, I have something I have to tell you," I say and swallow thickly, hating myself in this moment. I hate what I've become. How revenge and justice consumed me. My obsession changed who I was. For years.

I'm only vaguely aware of where we are and how someone could overhear, but I'm so afraid that if I don't tell him right now, I never will.

"Is it about what happened?" Dean asks me, his voice hard and I can only nod. The words pile up in the back of my throat, suffocating me. "Then you don't have to say it."

"You have to listen," I plead with him. "It's about me," I start to say, and my words come out scratchy as my throat closes. "It's my fault."

"You didn't make him hurt you." Dean's shoulders tense as he looks at me without holding back any emotion. The air turns bitter cold between us. "I don't care if you feel like you should have known. Fuck, I don't care if you were drunk and passed out naked with the door wide open." Dean's words are harsh as he lets the anger slip out. "I don't care if you blame yourself. I don't care if the world thinks you should have known. I don't give a fuck."

I worry my bottom lip between my teeth as tears prick my eyes.

"He didn't do it just once," Dean says and I can't hold back anything anymore.

I let out a hard, ugly sob, the images of Sam going up the stairs flashing through my mind. Shouldn't we have known back then? I wish we had. God, I swear I wish we had. "I want to take it back," I sob, barely getting out the words.

"Allie Cat, don't cry." Dean's words come out softly and he pulls me into his arms again.

"Please," I beg him as if he alone has the power to go back. I need him to listen. To hear me, and to understand.

He kisses my temple, my hair, rocking me as my tears slowly subside. I sniffle and try not to get his shirt wet and smeared with mascara, but he doesn't let me pull away.

"I'm not innocent," I tell Dean, looking him in the eyes and feeling the confession right there. "I'm telling you when I opened that door—"

"You let him in," Dean says and cuts me off. "That's all opening that door did. You let him in."

"I knew who he was." I let out the first part of the confession, the dark dirty secret spilling out in small pieces.

"All you did was let him in." He responds as if he didn't hear me.

I gave him the chance he needed. There's an evil in the eyes of those who cause pain. It won't be influenced. I should know. I knew when I opened that door that I was staring into the eyes of a man who would hurt me. And I welcomed him.

"I wanted him to come in. I wanted him to hurt me." My words are strangled, but Dean hears them.

His grip on me loosens as he looks down at me with an expression of disbelief, but it's quick to harden and he shakes his head.

"My friend Sam. He raped her," I say but have to stop and cover my mouth with my hand as I gasp for air. My eyes close as I try to calm myself down and Dean holds me, begging me to just come with him, but I need to get it out.

"Dean." I barely manage to look him in the eyes as I cling to his forearms and confess. "I came here knowing who he was. I wanted him to hurt me, so I could get justice for what he did to Sam." It's her name on my lips that makes my voice tremble and the tears fall. "I knew what I was doing, but I didn't want this."

Dean doesn't speak as the night gets colder and darker and a gust of wind pulls my hair behind my shoulder, baring my neck and letting the chill travel down my spine.

"So, if you want to run, I don't know that you'd really want me to be the one beside you. I'm not a good person, and I haven't been in so long. I hated him, Dean. I wanted him to pay ..."

Dean takes a step backward and the chill instantly replaces what's left of his warmth, but I can't stop myself from telling him everything.

"I came here," I say then pause as my vision clouds with tears and my shoulders shake. "I came here to set him up. I knew he would do it again ... not like that. I didn't know that would happen but I just had to give him the chance. It's my fault."

"He already had," Dean says although his gaze is vacant, and his words fall flat. "That girl in our class ... he already had."

"I didn't know," I say and then wipe under my eyes with the sleeves of my sweater. I can barely look Dean in the eyes.

"There's so much I didn't know. I didn't know I would meet you, let alone ..." I hesitate to admit what's between us. Or what was between us. It's odd, sensing the sickness of the truth being quickly replaced by emptiness. It's all that's left as I wait for Dean's judgment. But he doesn't say anything.

"Please talk to me." I have no right to speak to him, but I

still beg him. If he hates me, I'll deserve it.

"Say it," Dean commands me. "Tell me."

"Tell you what?" I grasp at anything I can to give Dean what he wants. "I didn't know I'd fall for you. I didn't think this would happen."

"You didn't think I'd kill him?" he asks as if he really thinks I'd set him up for that. I shake my head violently, praying that he'll believe me.

"Never. I never thought for one moment that you would get hurt."

"You thought you could let him hurt you like that and that I'd be okay?" he asks me, his eyes narrowed and his hands clench and unclench. He's on edge and for the first time, I'm scared.

"I thought you were done with me," I whisper and hearing the words and feeling the reality of them in this moment, makes a sharp pain tear through me, regret seeping into my veins.

"How could you ever think that?" Dean asks me in a single breath.

I can't answer. I don't have the words or the logic. "I just wanted him to pay for what he did to her." That's the truth. The need for him to get what he deserved outweighed everything else.

"I already knew, Allie," Dean says and swallows harshly as if he's the one confessing. "I had a lot of time in my cell to think. About what I knew about Kevin. About what I knew about you. Samantha Jenkins. She's the girl who claimed someone raped her at a party I was supposed to go to years ago. They never told us who the charges were against and I didn't know it was Kevin."

Disbelief grips me. He knows?

"I heard about it on the news when she killed herself but the details were missing and I was already so far gone ... but sitting in jail with nothing to do but think will help put the pieces together. The way you were with him that day outside the locker room ... I figured it out myself, Allie."

My eyes widen and I struggle to breathe. To say anything. He knew and he wants me? How could he?

"You will never do that again," Dean commands. "And you'll never talk about this again," he says and my breath halts. "Never tell anyone else. No one."

I nod my head, clasping my hands in front of me and with my posture as still as can be. My heart races and a flicker of hope lights inside of me. Dean looks at me for a long time, as if judging what he believes and what he finds lacking. *Please believe me.* My body trembles as I try not to grip on to him. As I wait for whatever it is he needs. Whatever it is, I'll give it to him.

"Is that everything?" he asks me. "Tell me now."

My bottom lip drops but I don't know what he's asking, or what he wants.

"What else are you hiding?" he asks in a raised voice and I cower as I shake my head and insist, "Nothing, nothing."

"You won't lie to me again." His voice is hard.

I almost tell him that I never lied, but that wouldn't be true. I kept the truth from him, and that action in and of itself was a lie.

"Is there anyone else that you *want* to hurt you?" he asks me, and I can't stand the anger that's there. "Because I swear to God I don't know what I'll do if anyone tries to hurt you."

"No. No. I'm sorry," I tell him in a croak, shame washing over me.

"Do you realize what could have happened? What he would have done to you?" Dean asks and his own voice cracks.

"Not until he was," I start to say and remember how heavy his body was, how much it hurt.

My eyes squeeze shut tight, but not tight enough. I just want it all to go away. "I wish I could take it back. I'm so sorry."

"I would do it again, Allie. I'd kill anyone who tried to hurt you."

"I didn't mean for that to happen."

"Don't keep anything from me, do you hear me?" he asks me, and his voice is consoling this time.

"I promise," I tell him with all sincerity. "I have no more secrets."

"Good, because I still love you. I love you, Allison."

I finally breathe, a large gulp of air that's nearly too much as I fall into him. His arms wrap around me tightly, holding me just as fiercely as I hold him.

"And I want you to come with me." His words are

whispered into my hair.

I can only nod, I can't speak anymore. I have nothing left to give, but if I ever I do, it's all for Dean.

Before I'm ready, Dean pulls me away from him, letting the cold air come between us and for a moment, I think he's changing his mind. But then he speaks.

"Just don't stop loving me," he says as he stares deeply into my eyes.

"Never," I breathe out the word quickly, desperate for him to know how true it is. I love him. I love him more than he'll ever know.

Chapter 38

Dean

"How many boxes?" I ask Allie as I pull the clear packaging tape down the center of the box.

"Fourteen," she tells me, appearing from the kitchen doorway with a cup of tea in her hands. "It all fit in fourteen boxes," she says, leaning her hip against the wall and then blowing over the cup.

She kept the empty cardboard boxes, breaking them down and stacking them neatly in the pantry. Like she knew she was going to need them before long.

Every time I'm reminded of why she came here, the very thing that brought her to me, my chest aches with a pain that runs deep. A pain I don't think will ever leave me.

"You sure you don't want a cup?" Her small voice carries into the room and snaps me out of the dark thought.

When I glance up at her, ready to say no again, the hint of happiness is on her face. Or maybe it's hope. With her hair draped over her shoulders and wearing nothing but a pair of panties and one of my old rugby shirts, she looks perfect. The shirt clings to the middle of her waist when she stands like that. Everything about her makes me want to take her into my arms and never let go.

Partly because she needs it, but mostly because I need her.

"Maybe I will," I tell her and drop the roll of tape on the floor, turning the box upright. We have two boxes packed and within just a few hours, Allie's place will be cleared out. I want to pretend we were never here and rewrite our story, but that's life. You don't get to rewrite it.

As I stand, my back cracks and my stiff neck and shoulders ache. I haven't slept for shit, not since I got out of jail and I don't think I will again until we leave this place, this city ... all of it. A fresh start is what we want and need. Wherever that might take us.

Her bare feet pad against the floor as she heads back into the kitchen.

I follow the sound of her running the faucet and then opening and closing the microwave. She's in front of it, gripping the counter and staring absently ahead when I walk in.

"Allie Cat." I barely speak her name. Her green eyes

search for mine instantly. Every time I move or speak, she's there waiting for me, on edge and waiting for something. That's the way it's been since I've been back here. It's like she's afraid I'm going to run or that one day I'll wake up and think she isn't worth it. That loving her costs too much. It fucking kills me. I'll hold her and love her every day until she knows I'm here for good and staying.

She doesn't know what lies ahead, and neither do I.

But I know it'll be all right, so long as she's with me.

In three strides I'm beside her, silencing the microwave with the mug of water in it for tea and pulling her into my arms instead.

"I want to hear you tell me you're all right," I whisper, cupping her chin in my hand and forcing her eyes to mine. She doesn't have a trace of makeup on and under her eyes are dark circles, although she's been sleeping all right; better than she was before.

"I couldn't be with you because I didn't want to be okay and you made me so much more than just okay."

"You know I love you," I tell her. It's not the first or second or third time I've told her since I've come home to her. And I'll keep telling her until the look in her green eyes reflects that she knows they're true.

"I love you," she says back in barely a whisper, her expression changing to one of complete sincerity but also laced with pain. Her eyes close as she lets out a breath and presses her cheek into my hand.

I knew she was hiding something and that's what drew me to her. From the very beginning, she was a mystery.

The dark secrets I didn't expect. Who could've ever expected this?

Allie peeks up at me, the hurt and worry still in her eyes.

She's walking on eggshells. She's been this way for days and I hate myself for even feeling slightly angry toward her.

Even though she should have told me.

I love her.

I'd kill again for her. And she knows I would.

Sitting in that cell with nothing to do but think on how it came down to this, the pieces slowly fell into place.

The reason why she kept pushing me away even though we both knew we fit together just right.

The reason she seemed off to me when I first met her, the reason I was drawn to her.

It was meant to be this way. As tragic and horrific as it is. I should have been at that party to stop it, but fate found another way, the two of us too broken to prevent the pain. I'll take her however I can have her.

"Come sit with me?" I ask her and she's quick to give me the trace of a smile when I take her small hand in mine. She's eager to make things right and to make me happy, I can feel it in everything she does. Every small look and move is cautious and eager to please.

I sit cross-legged on the floor of the dining room. The sofa's already in the truck, so the barren floor will have to do.

"When did you become so shy, Allie Cat?" I ask her as she settles in my lap.

"Shy?"

"I feel like you're hiding from me," I tell her honestly.

"I'm just ..."

"Ashamed?" I say the word I hate to think is the truth.

"And afraid," she tells me softly in a single breath.

"Of what?"

"I don't want to lose you, but I know I don't deserve you." Thank God she's at least confessed what I already knew.

"You're wrong." My heart beats quicker, my blood runs warmer. All from fear of losing her. I swear I'll never let her run again.

"I never meant for you to get hurt," she tells me again. I don't know why she feels the need. I believe her. Every word.

"I think it was supposed to happen this way," I say and pull her soft body closer to mine. "I'm not mad at what you did." I'm careful with my words as I add, "I'm upset you didn't tell me but I'm not mad, and I don't hold any of this against you."

She only nods her head, casting her gaze down and picking at the hem of the shirt she's wearing. My shirt. "What I did wasn't okay," she whispers.

I force her chin up with my hand on her jaw. "You only did it because something had to be done."

"I did it out of anger," she's quick to admit. As if acting out of anger made her intentions worse.

"You did it out of pain," I say.

Her eyes water and she closes them, not wanting to cry in front of me. Or maybe not wanting to cry at all anymore.

"I'm sorry about Sam, and I'm not sorry that Kevin's dead."

"I'm not sorry he's dead either," she says, closing her eyes and letting the tears seep into her thick lashes.

"I love you, Allison. I love you so fucking much. And it kills me that you never told me."

"I didn't know if you'd believe me," she says, and it cuts through my heart. "But I also didn't want you to stop me." That's the real truth. And I get it. I understand it. I still hate it, though. "She needed this. Sam needed this," she says and then breaks down in my arms.

"Where do we go from here?" I ask her. We want each other. But there's no roadmap for what the future holds and that's terrifying for her.

"Forgive me, and I'll go wherever you want. I'll run away forever. I'll do whatever you want," she says, brushing the tears away and leaving her cheeks reddened.

A heavy breath leaves me in a huff. "I've already forgiven you, Allie."

"I love you. I'm so sorry," she says hurriedly.

"Stop saying you're sorry." I plant a small kiss on her lips, tasting the hint of salt from her tears. "And I love you too," I whisper against her lips.

A moment passes before she questions me.

"You really love me? Even still?" she asks me, and I hate that she questions it.

"Of course I do." I brush my knuckles across her cheek and gently push the hair out of her face. "That's not something I can stop," I say before lowering my lips to hers.

She softens, eagerly accepting my kiss and parting her mouth for more.

"Please don't stop," she tells me when I pull away and at first, I think she means the kiss, but then she adds, "I can't lose you ..." Her voice skips and she takes in a quick breath. "I don't know what I would do if you stopped loving me."

"I never will," I tell her with a small smile playing on my lips. My voice is upbeat, but it doesn't echo what I feel. That first day I saw her in class, a piece of me recognized something inside of her and now that I have it, I can't lose it. I can't lose her.

"You love me and I love you. That's all we need," I say, and she doesn't know how raw my promise is.

She rises from her seated position, crashing her lips against mine with a desperate need.

For forgiveness. For love. For a life without pain and regret.

Her grip is tight as her nails scratch through my hair as she intensifies the kiss. For the first time in days, I want more. I want to feel every bit of her. I want to give her everything and make her mine again.

She parts the seam of her lips, granting me entry and I'm instantly hard for her. Desperate for more of her to be bared to me.

She only pulls back from our kiss to breathe.

"Please," she says and nuzzles against me. "I need you." Her voice is laced with anguish.

Her small hands slip under my shirt. They're warm and her fingers are gentle as she moves them to my back, eager to touch every inch of me.

"I need you," she says again, her eyes wide and pleading. "I need to feel you," she adds. She kisses the little dip at the bottom of my throat and then my neck.

It's been tense between us but more than that, I haven't touched her since everything's changed.

"Please," she whispers with need and I'm quick move her out of my lap and lay her on the floor, my hands moving under her shirt to her hips, looping around the thin panties and pulling them slowly down her thighs.

Her eyes are closed, her lips parted as she pants.

It doesn't take me long to strip down and settle myself between her thighs, all the while leaving kisses along her jaw, her neck, that little dip beneath her collarbone. Every inch of her skin that I can kiss, I do.

"I love you," she murmurs over and over, and when her eyes finally open and reach mine, she says it with a strength that can't be denied.

I slam into her, filling her completely in one swift stroke. Her bare back rubs along the hardwood floor as I thrust into her, again and again. It's an unrelenting pace. Her head thrashes and her eyes close tight as I grip her hips and pin her down.

I have to brace her to take the force of my thrusts.

She's so tight, so wet.

Her gasp is coarse; her nails dig into my wrists. With her eyes shut tight, her body tenses. She shakes her head and I know this is wrong.

She's thinking about it.

About what happened.

"Allie," I murmur and brace my arm behind her back, pulling her up to sit on top of me. I kiss her ravenously with her on top of me. "Look at me," I command her and instantly her eyes open. She holds on to me with a fierceness, wrapping her arms around my shoulders and burying her head in the crook of my neck. Emotions or her memories getting the best of her.

I wasn't sure how she would react after what transpired, but holding her now, I hate it. I hate that she's not lost in pleasure and that the thoughts of what one man did to her have dared to come between us.

I stay as still as I can, still buried inside of her, but not wanting to move yet.

"Look at me," I tell her again more firmly and she does slowly.

"I'm sorry, I thought I could ..." her voice trails off and her shame comes back, but it's gone the moment my words hit her.

"You're mine." I say the words reverently, our shared gaze heating with raw vulnerability. "No one else will ever touch you." My heart beats hard and heavy, but slowly. "I'll take it all away."

"And you're mine," she says and runs her fingers through my hair. Her touch gentle but possessive. I love it.

With her on top of me, I move my hands to her hips and rock her. Our eyes still locked. Her clit pressing against me with every motion.

"Slow at first," I tell her and pump my hips once, burying myself inside her, but still letting her lead. She gasps a moan as her hands fall on my chest. Her small fingers dig into my shoulders.

She nips my bottom lip, letting the tip of her nose brush against mine as she pulls away slightly, but rocks her hips again, making her body shudder with pleasure.

My hand moves to the back of her head, and only then does she look at me. "We'll get through this," I tell her, searching her eyes to make damn sure she believes me. "I've got you."

Whatever she asks for and however she needs it, that's how it will always be with us.

Always and forever.

Epilogue

Allison

"How are things going now that you're settled in?" Dr. Robinson asks me. I like his office; it's cozy with the dark furniture and a thick rug under my feet. I like it more when Dean's with me.

"Well, really well," I answer, letting out an easy breath as I pick my feet up and slip them under me to get comfortable.

"Moving was a good change, a new environment for both of us."

"So everything went smoothly?"

"Better than I thought. Daniel took over the lease at the place I'd been renting."

"And Daniel is Dean's friend?" he asks me.

"Yeah, he's a good guy," I say and my heart races as I talk. Because I'm hiding the truth. I'm keeping what I overheard just yesterday to myself. Daniel has his own demons, but that's not my story to tell. It's his and he'll get through it. I know he will.

He nods in approval although he doesn't write anything. The book stays on his lap, the pen sitting on top. My eyes keep flickering to it; I always wonder which parts of our session Dr. Robinson deems worthy of recording.

"We got a golden retriever," I tell him. "He's just a fluffy puppy, but he's sweet."

"You got him together?" he asks me.

"My mother got him for us."

"And how does that make you feel?"

"You sound like a shrink when you ask me that," I tell him.

"And you sound like you're deflecting." He's quick to call me on my shit.

My eyes fall on the coffee table and I feel a tug at my heartstrings. "I feel like he's too good for me." I speak without looking up at Dr. Robinson, but the telltale sign of his leather notebook opening makes me huff a small laugh. I guess anything that hurts my heart is worthy.

"My grandmother used to say, find someone who loves you just a little more than you love them." My eyes water, remembering how she said it. And how she meant it.

"And is that how you view your relationship with Dean?"

he asks me.

I shake my head, nearly violently, as I wipe the tears away from the corners of my eyes. "No," I say quickly, the word coming out scratchy. "But I'm afraid that's how he'll feel because I'm not good at loving anymore. That's what really matters. It's not about the truth. It's all about what people think."

"Why do you say that?" he asks me.

"Because it's so obvious he'd do anything for me. And I'm scared he doesn't think I'd do the same for him." I would. *I'd kill for him, die for him. Dean is my everything.*

"No, why do you say you aren't good at loving anymore?" Dr. Robinson says. He adds before I can answer, "Dean knows you love him. It's something that's clear to him. And to me,."

It soothes me like a balm on my aching chest, calming the anxiety and nerves that keep me up at night. "Why do you think you're not good at loving?"

"I haven't done it before. Not like this. And I'm scared," I say, the confession coming out in a single breath.

"Scared of what?" he asks me.

"That one day he'll leave me, and I won't survive it." I sniff, reaching for the tissues on the coffee table and keep talking without looking him in the eyes.

"I don't know how he can forgive me so easily. He says it's love, but I still don't quite feel like I deserve it."

"Because you were protecting yourself."

"If I had trusted him sooner," I start to say the same thing

I've been saying for weeks. I stop myself and pick under my nails, staring blindly ahead. "I can't change the past."

"And your past is where it belongs, behind you. What you have now is someone who loves you and who you love in return. Someone who wants to grow with you. Someone who knows the shadow side of yourself and you know his. There isn't much that could be more ideal than that. To love and be loved for every part of you."

"I feel like I can never show Dean how much I love him."

"Maybe that's a good thing. I want that to be your homework."

"What?"

"I want you to write down ways you show Dean how you love him and how he loves you."

I nod my head easily, feeling relieved slightly. Even if I could write it all down, Dean will never know exactly what he means to me. He knows everything, my darkest secrets, and he still loves me, without judgment. He gave me a new life and it's complete with him in it.

I don't think it's possible to feel more love for that man than I do.

"Do you believe in fate, Dr. Robinson?" I speak without thinking.

"Why do you ask?" he answers my question with a question of his own and a small laugh bubbles up as I trace the edge of the coffee table with my fingers. It's hard and unforgiving as I let my thoughts surface without fear of his judgment.

"Dean was supposed to be at that party." It takes a moment for the good doctor to realize what I'm saying and when he does, his brow raises with surprise.

"If he hadn't gotten suspended and in that fight with his stepdad, he would have been there."

"And what do you think about that?" Dr. Robinson asks me.

"I think he would have hit it off with Sam." My answer comes out choked.

"Do you think he would have ended up with her and not you?"

"I think none of it would have happened." The words pour from me. "I don't think any of that night would have happened." The thought of that night being erased eases a pain inside of me, but then it comes back full force knowing that wish will never come true.

"Maybe we were supposed to be together, like fate."

"Or soulmates," he says.

"Whatever you want to call it." I shrug and then add, "Maybe that's why we felt the way we did toward each other when I first came here. Like somewhere deep down inside we knew, and Dean knew it long before me because he wasn't as broken."

"Do you still feel broken?" Dr. Robinson asks me and it's such a ridiculous question.

"Of course I am." Once you're shattered, you can be mended but the cracks are still there. "Both of us were flawed, but together we make sense, don't we?" I ask Dr. Robinson, and never in my life has someone's judgment meant more to me. He simply nods as his timer goes off.

It's time to go.

Time for a fresh start.

About the Author

Thank you so much for reading my romances. I'm just a stay at home Mom and an avid reader turned Author and I couldn't be happier.

I hope you love my books as much as I do!

More by Willow Winters
www.willowwinterswrites.com/books

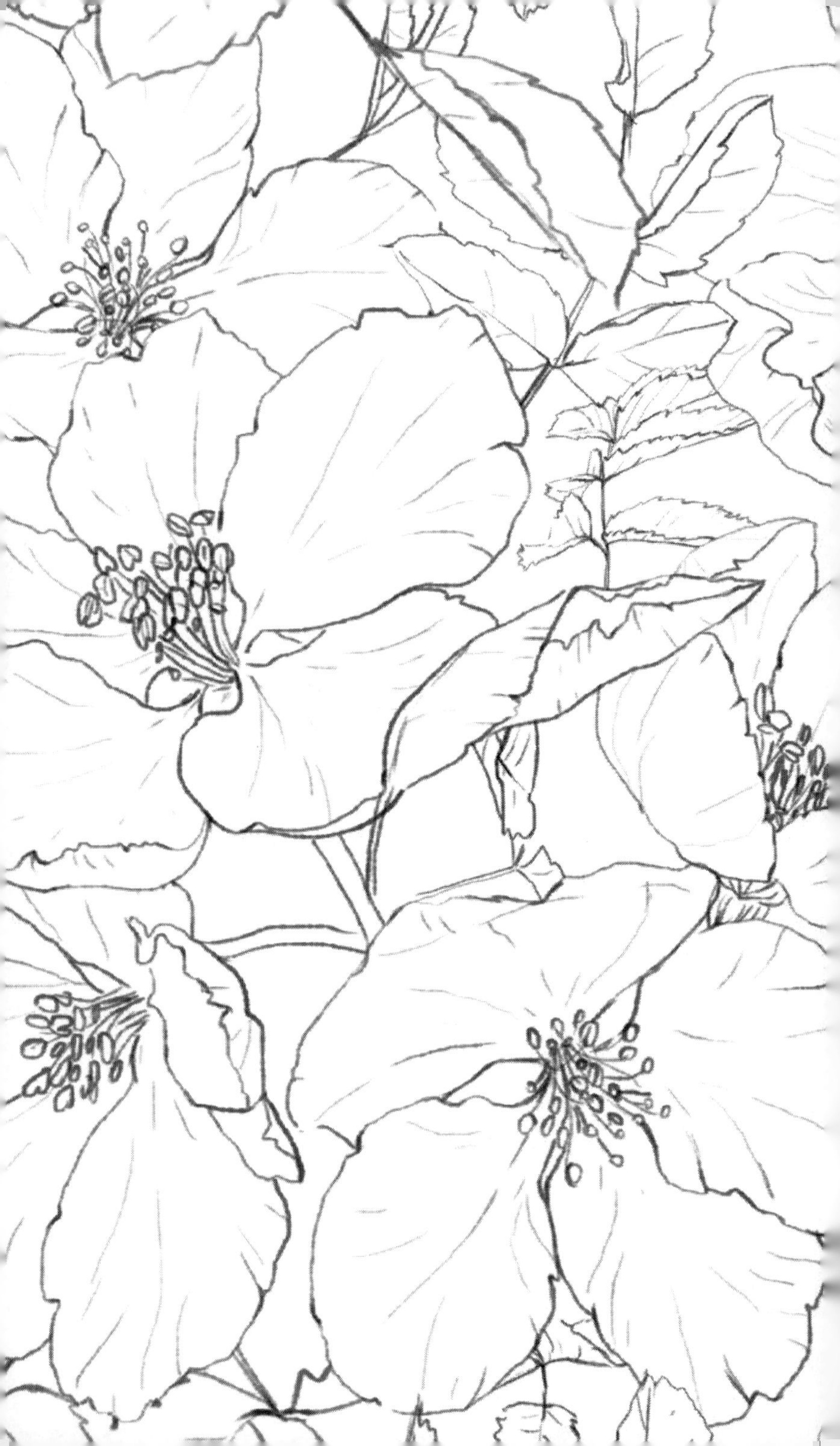

Printed in Great Britain
by Amazon